Sweet & Spicy

A SWEET WATER NOVEL

SAMANTHA WHISKEY

D1518236

Content Warning

This book contains some depictions of emotional abuse and physical abuse (off page and through memory), sexual assault, addiction recovery, and sexual content. I've taken every precaution to handle these issues sensitively, but if any of these situations could be considered triggering to you, please take note.

Also by Samantha Whiskey

Now Available on Audio!

CAROLINA REAPERS SERIES
Spicy southern nights meets the chill of the ice in this hot hockey romance series!

Axel

Sawyer

Connell

Logan

Cannon

SEATTLE SHARKS SERIES
Let the Sharks spice up your commute!

Grinder

Enforcer

Winger

Rookie

ROYAL ROMANCE SERIES
These twin princes are sure to help you escape!

The Crown

The Throne

To those who need to be loved a little harder

CHAPTER 1

Anne

"Would you like to talk more about your sister's wedding?" Dr. Casson asked me from where she sat in the cushioned arm chair across from me.

As far as therapists went, she was already the best one I'd ever been to. She owned her own office in my hometown of Sweet Water, South Carolina, and she kept her space cozy with rich, warm furniture, and walls lined with books and cute knickknacks that screamed of lazy days browsing antiques.

"Andromeda?" she asked, and I blinked out of my thoughts.

"Please call me Anne," I said, not for the first time.

Andromeda VanDoren was what my family called me.

Andromeda was the person I never wanted to be.

It'd been three weeks since my sister Persephone had gotten married.

Three weeks since I'd hit another rock bottom with the massive train wreck that was my life.

Three weeks since I'd finally asked for help.

"Right, Anne," she said, giving me a soft smile that definitely suited her demeanor. Dr. Zoe Casson exuded the perfect combination of intelligence and warmth. "Would you like to talk about the wedding again?"

I shook my head. "I think we covered that the first two weeks I was here."

Shame ricocheted in my body, making my heart clench. The first two weeks here were brutal, to say the least. I'd confessed to my rotten behavior regarding my sister and her new NHL star of a husband, and told Dr. Casson all about my inability to see past old trauma when it came to my sister—not that I told her what that trauma *was*, I wasn't ready yet—but she understood all the same. I'd apologized to Persephone and her husband Cannon weeks ago, but that didn't wash away my sins.

And what was truly awful?

Those sins weren't even the worst of what I'd done.

I'd done a hundred times worse over the last decade, often times not even remembering my actions the next morning. My life was a series of mistakes, all birthed from one blip in time I couldn't seem to outrun.

But I was here.

I was trying.

I didn't want to be a mistake anymore.

I didn't want to be the person who brought my family down.

I didn't want to die.

As if on cue, exhaustion settled heavy in my bones and I sank deeper into the chair.

"Okay," Dr. Casson said, nodding slightly, her caramel and brown hair falling over her forehead. "How is your mother's recovery going?"

I breathed a sigh of relief, genuine happiness lifting my spirits. "She's recovering beautifully," I said.

She'd gotten a lifesaving kidney transplant two days after

Persephone's wedding, and she was already home. The doctors were giving her glowing reviews, praising her perfect patient behavior. She took her meds on time, ate a steady and healthy diet, and rested as much as possible. They told her in another five weeks she'd be able to resume her normal activities.

"Her body accepted the transplant without a hitch," I continued, unable to contain my smile.

But right alongside the joy was a brutal stab of pain and guilt.

I'd tried to get tested to see if I would be a proper match for a donor—even though most of my family thought I'd selfishly refused. If I would've been a match I would've offered my kidney up on a silver platter, but my *life choices* prevented me from even getting that far.

Thanks to years of non-stop drinking and partying, my liver was on the verge of failing. Toxic hepatitis with a fun side-effect of cirrhosis was how they explained it. If I didn't stop drinking, stop partying, I wouldn't live to see another birthday.

Of course, I'd stopped.

I didn't *want* to die, even though it would make my family's life so much easier.

Three weeks sober and counting. It wasn't easy. Not after years of creating habits that revolved around my next mental escape, but I was managing. It didn't hurt that my sister had found the best phycologist in town to fit me into her over-crowded schedule, and as long as I met the expectations of my family—which included random alcohol and drug tests, among other things—they wouldn't force me into a rehabilitation clinic.

Not that they could technically *force* me, but I didn't need an intervention.

I needed a fucking miracle if I was expected to get my life together.

One step at a time.

"You mentioned last week that even though you and your sister are on better terms, you still have a hard time trusting her?"

I swallowed the knot in my throat.

"It's not just her," I admitted, shifting in my seat to fiddle with the end of my dress. It was one of those beautiful November days in South Carolina that felt more like spring than fall. Tonight, the temps would drop, but for now I was basking in it.

"Who else?"

"My entire family, really," I said, forcing myself to be honest.

Dr. Casson told me during my first session there would be no point in lying to her—she had a talent for sniffing them out. She'd further said that being honest was the only way she could help me heal, help me do better.

And I really, really wanted to do better.

I didn't like being a mess. It wasn't like I thrived in the misery of a string of failed marriages that were more impulsive than one-clicking an online sale or the countless times I'd picked the wrong man and ended up on the wrong side of his hand.

It wasn't like I enjoyed hurting my family, hurting my sister...

"You look so much like her tonight," he said, backing me into a corner. "If I ask really nice, will you let me call you by her name?"

A wave of nausea crashed in my stomach, and I tried to breathe around it.

"What is it about them that makes them hard to trust?" she asked.

"I suppose you could trace it back to how we were raised. Being a VanDoren isn't as easy as it likely seems to the public.

Mistakes aren't tolerated and if you *did* make them...if you ran into a situation where you needed help, you were better off pretending it never happened."

Dr. Casson nodded while she twirled her pen in her hand. "So you felt like you couldn't go to them for help."

I nodded.

"And now?"

"Now..." I blew out a breath. "Persephone and I are getting reacquainted as sisters." The notion brought a soft smile to my lips.

I loved my sister, but our past...well, *my* past was complicated. She was oblivious to the source of indifference that had festered between us for far too long. And yes, that was my fault. I never talked to her about what happened, never really dealt with what happened, instead choosing to try and drink the memory away or outrun it.

But I was here now. Trying.

"Is there anyone besides your sister that you're reconnecting with? Any member of your family that makes you feel safe enough to trust them? Talk to them openly?"

"No," I admitted. "I want to reach that place at some point with my parents, but they've never really understood me."

"Can you elaborate on that a bit?"

I folded my hands in my lap to keep from gripping the armrest of the chair. "We're only eighteen months apart," I explained. "My sister and me. I don't remember a time when my baby sister wasn't the most important thing in the world to me. To my entire family, really. Growing up, everything came so effortlessly to her. She was elegant and poised in diapers, or so my mother tells me. But me? I was the tough one. The complicated one. Too emotional. Too impulsive. Too combative." I shook my head. "Some of my earliest memories are of my parents begging me not to make a scene at some charity event while at the same time praising Persephone for being so delightfully quiet and polite. One of the times I remember was when I was seven. I hadn't made a scene, I'd just asked when the food would be served."

Tears pricked the back of my eyes, but I tipped my chin and forced them down. "I'm not saying instances like those excuse my recent behavior," I hurried to add. "But you can only be told you're the problem child so many times before you decide to live up to title."

"That's understandable," she said. "And it must've made the relationship between you and your sister very strained growing up."

I shrugged. "I adored her. She's impossible not to love. And none of it was her fault. She didn't ask to be perfect. She didn't ask for our parents to constantly shame me and praise her. I never really started feeling the disdain for her until—" I stopped myself short, swallowing hard.

I was *so* not going there today.

A knowing look flashed in Dr. Casson's rich brown eyes, but she must've seen my determination and pivoted. "Can you remember a time you did fully trust someone? In your family or outside of it. Can you remember the last time someone made you feel safe to just be you and not who your parents wanted you to be?"

"Do you think if we climbed on these tables and screamed at the top of our lungs that anyone in here would notice?" I asked, whispering in Jim's ear as we sat in our designated spots in our high school's cafeteria.

His light green eyes flashed as he looked at me before scanning the cafeteria. It was packed with the entire junior class, all stoically silent and listening aptly to a guest speaker from some corporation or another. There had been three of these this week already and I was so bored.

"Feeling a little restless?" he asked, and warmth shot through my veins.

Jim and I were only in the flirting stages of our relationship, but heaven help me I couldn't get enough of this boy.

"That," I said. "But also, I don't think any of them would bat an eye. They'd never jeopardize their future by giving attention to an outburst." I practically radiated my father when I spoke the words.

Jim laughed, and I couldn't help but look at his full lips. God, I bet he was a great kisser.

"Don't worry," I hurried to say. "I won't corrupt you." I was here because my parents wanted me in the most prestigious private school available. Jim was here on a scholarship. One strike and he'd be sent packing.

"If you want to get up on these tables and scream, I'm right there with you." A smirk shaped his lips, the kind that made my heart flutter.

"Really?" I asked, mystified by the boy who never seemed to care about my wild tendencies, didn't criticize me for getting lost in the music and dancing wherever I heard it, didn't chide me for spicing up our strict uniforms with whatever accessories I could sneak past the uptight school admins.

Jim cocked an eyebrow at me, his smile infectious as he stood up halfway from his seat, placing his hands on the table like he was about to climb on top of it.

I grabbed him and hauled him back down, barely suppressing the giggle bubbling in my chest. A few people glanced our way, but dutifully ignored us.

"You're ridiculous," I whispered, downright beaming at him.

He shrugged, eying the hand I still had on his forearm. "I may be ridiculous," he said. "But so are you. And in a place like this?" he nodded toward the stoic room. "I think that means you're stuck with me."

"Anne?" Dr. Casson's voice pushed me out of the memory. "Where did you go just now."

I blinked a few times, hating that the memory felt like a warm blanket and a dream all at the same time.

"There was someone," I said. "Once. In high school."

"Oh?" she asked, grinning. "An old flame?"

"You could say that."

"And how did this person make you feel safe?"

"He liked me for exactly who I was." I sighed, relaxing a bit in the chair. "He never asked me to change."

And he never, not once, compared me to Persephone.

"And what happened with him?"

"My father didn't approve of our relationship," I said, shoving down the flickering pain from the old wound. "Jim's father passed away when he was a kid, and his mother barely made ends meet waiting tables. He wasn't exactly what my father viewed as VanDoren relationship material."

"Ouch." Dr. Casson furrowed her brow. "Did you ever reach out to him after you were out of your parent's control?"

I laughed at that. "I've never been out of my parent's control. To this day they use my inheritance like a bargaining chip. Besides, I'm sure he's married with four children and a pair of chocolate labs by now. Probably has a white picket fence and everything."

I looked down at my nails, pretending to examine them while she studied me. I didn't want her to see the regret shining in my eyes. Didn't want her to see the pain I felt over never trying to reconnect with him. But in the end, it was for the best that my father tore us apart.

I would've ruined his life.

That's what I did, what I've always done.

"Is there anything wrong with white picket fences and a simple life?"

I finally returned my focus to her.

"No," I said. "There's nothing wrong with that. Nothing at all."

* * *

I didn't know how badly my feet could hurt before I started waiting tables at *Lyla's Place*, one of the most popular restaurants in Sweet Water. They practically barked at me after my shift.

Darkness had settled over the town, the sky an inky black splattered with diamonds as I sat in my car, stalling as the thought of driving home to my empty studio apartment. I wasn't used to being alone, even if the company I used to keep wasn't exactly healthy for me. The idea of sitting in the silence with myself made me want to scream. Or cry. Maybe both. Today's session had certainly opened up a box I'd kept locked up for a decade, and it was like I couldn't *stop* feeling everything.

Feeling sad, regretful, ashamed, embarrassed, pissed off. I ping-ponged from each emotion all night, all while wearing my proper southern smile like a mask while I waited on customers.

It was too much.

I *felt* too much.

It swarmed me, all the emotions filling me up from the inside out like grains of sand until I was sure I'd suffocate from it. It made everything harder—thinking, breathing.

Maybe it was normal to feel all these things at once.

Maybe it only felt strange to me because I usually floated in the wonderful space of oblivion provided by alcohol.

Thirst swept over me, and I glanced to my right, eying the small bottle in the cup holder.

I'd bought it in a low moment last week.

My fingers itched to crack the lid. One drink wouldn't kill me.

Only, it could.

Right. It could. Was the numbing fog it offered worth dying over?

Would anyone even miss me? They'd probably be so relieved. I could see them at my funeral, teary eyed but content knowing they didn't have to deal with me anymore.

The bottle was in my hands without me even realizing it, the lid partially cracked open.

Fuck it.

I opened it completely, bringing it to my lips, the harsh smell hitting my nose—

"No," I said to myself. "No, I don't want to be this person anymore. I don't." My hands shook, the clear liquid in the bottle sloshing slightly. "I'm stronger than this. I'm a VanDoren for Christ's sake."

I hurriedly put the cap back on and started the car, suddenly desperate to get home and dump this down the drain. I pulled onto the road, swerving slightly as the bottle in my lap tipped and liquid spilled onto my pants.

"Damn it," I groaned, trying my best to scoop up the bottle with one hand and drive with the other. I obviously didn't get the lid screwed on tight enough, and trying to do it one-handed wasn't exactly easy.

Luckily the traffic was light—

Something small and black darted out in front of me, a flash of light blinking off a reflective surface. I slammed on my breaks and swerved off the road to avoid hitting it. The bottle flew out of my hands, upturning and dumping its entire contents all over my shirt.

I threw the car in park, my hands shaking from the jump scare.

"What in the absolute hell?" I said, glancing down at

myself now covered in the exact drink I was trying to stay away from. "Perfect."

A whining sound rang outside my car, and I leaned up over the steering wheel to see over the hood of my car, silently praying I hadn't hit anything. Relief crashed over me when I spotted the culprit of the whole mess—a midnight-black cat with its head stuck in some sort of plastic container, the poor thing.

It jerked its head back and forth, ferally mewing as it tried to get the thing off.

I unbuckled my seatbelt, and hurried out of the car, but that made the little thing speed off in the opposite direction.

"Well, now I can't help you if you run away!" I said to the cat like it would understand me, then stamped my foot for good measure. I was soaked, my feet hurt, and I was pissed at myself for even buying the bottle of alcohol now seeping into my clothes. I wanted nothing more than a good bath and a long sleep. But I couldn't leave it like this.

I spotted it across the street, darting under one of the vacant houses that lined the road, and hurried to follow it. Using the light from my phone, I found a gap underneath the dilapidated porch and knelt to find the cat curled up and hissing through the plastic jar on its head.

"Talk to me like that again and I'll leave you here to be forever known as the cat in the jar."

It glared at me.

Well, the attitude matched the vibe.

There was no grass to speak of, just mud that I crawled through as I wedged myself into the hole, reaching for the cat as best I could. I could kiss these clothes goodbye, which normally wouldn't bother me, but since my parents had cut me off, I had very little to my name and I needed these pants for work.

"You see this mess you've gotten us into?" I chided the cat, wiggling under the porch a little more. Gracious, it smelled like old wood and dirt and I tried really hard not to think about all the bugs that were likely waiting to feast on my skin like an all-you-can-eat buffet. "Now, come here and I'll help you."

The cat didn't move. In fact, it looked like it would bite my head off if it weren't for the jar currently muzzling it.

"Fine, suit yourself." I reached, finally able to grab hold of its neck fur, and dragged it toward me. I moved backward, knowing I needed more space in order to remove the jar without hurting it.

I made it halfway before a creaking sound cracked through the air, and half the porch slumped to my left, squeezing against my hips. I cringed, bracing for pain, but thankfully, the impact was slow, almost lazy in its crumbling. After realizing I hadn't been properly crushed because of some random cat, I blew out a breath and tried to move again.

Only I couldn't.

I tried again, my hips hitting a tighter squeeze in the wood now that it'd crumbled.

I flailed my legs, trying frantically to gain purchase and shake my body free of the space.

Nothing worked.

I shook my head, looking at the cat in my arms. "Are you happy now?" I snapped. "We're totally, fully *stuck*."

CHAPTER 2

Jim

"Are you sure there isn't anyone in there?" Barbara asked me as I motioned for her to go back inside her house.

"I checked the entire property," I assured her. "There's no one in there but your dog."

The elderly woman nodded, frowning as her eyes shifted to the side like she was trying to remember something but couldn't quite reach it. "I swore I heard something in the back room."

I gave her a soft smile. "Let's go check it one more time together, okay?"

"Yes," she said. "That would be nice."

I took her arm, helping steady her as we walked through her tiny but cozy house. Tonight was a bad night for Mrs. Jensen. She didn't remember me when I showed up after she'd called the department with claims of an intruder. I'd answered the same call twice already this week, and would likely answer it again next week.

She suffered from late-stage dementia, and some days were harder than others. She'd been friends with my grandmother,

13

back when her and my parents were still alive. Barbara's family lived across the country, but they made sure she had in-home care when she refused to be put in a nursing home.

Only problem was, the in-home care wasn't live-in, and so nights were always hit or miss. I made sure to check on her every week, ensuring she had plenty of groceries and dog food. Mainly, I think she just liked it when I came over so she had someone to talk to, which is why I made my trips a weekly thing.

But the calls had nothing to do with me. She would've been fine with any officer coming to investigate her claim since she couldn't remember me right now, and that was fine. What was most important was helping her feel safe in her home.

"See," I said, walking her through the back room and showing her every opened closet door. I even showed her that I checked under the bed. "All clear. The back door hasn't been tampered with, nor the front. All windows are locked and secure. It's just you and Dane here." I patted the retriever mix at my feet, the old dog wagging its tail as he looked up at me.

"He's certainly taken with you," she said. "He doesn't normally like strangers."

My heart clenched for her, but I made sure to smile and nod. "He's a good boy," I said. "And he's still got a great pair of ears on him. He knew the second I pulled into the drive. He'll tell you if anything is amiss, but you know you can call us anytime."

She smiled up at me, relief pooling in her eyes. "Thank you," she said. "I know it's late. Do you want some iced tea for the road?"

It was only nine thirty, and my night was just getting started. Not that Sweet Water had a ton of criminal activity, but there was enough work to go around and I'd picked up a couple night shifts this week since I wouldn't be able to next week. I'd be heading up a refresher course for new recruits for the next six weeks and that meant a steadier schedule for a little while. I wasn't mad about it because it would be a nice change from constantly switching shifts.

"No, thank you," I said as I headed out her front door.

She lingered in her opened doorway as I turned around to say goodbye.

"Oh!" she said suddenly. "Jim, it's just always a delight when you come over. Thank you for visiting me."

"Pleasure is all mine, Barbara," I said, nodding to her as I waved goodbye and headed to my cruiser. I sank behind the wheel, waiting to make sure she went back inside her house before I started it up.

"Officer Harlowe?" Dispatch rang over my radio. "We've had some calls about a drunk driver off the side of twenty-seven over there by *Lyla's Place*. Can you respond?"

"Officer Harlowe in route to twenty-seven," I said into my radio down before hitting the road. Drunk drivers weren't unheard of in Sweet Water, but they were definitely rare. "Has there been an accident?" I asked once on the road.

"No, sir," dispatch said. "But one of the callers said the woman driving swerved off the road and then jumped out of the car and ran across the street."

I furrowed my brow. "Copy that."

It only took me five minutes to pull up on location, thanks to Sweet Water being so small. I easily spotted the vacant car on the side of the road, parked behind it, and hopped out.

A muffled groan sounded from my left, and I pulled out my torch, shining the light across the street at the sound.

"What in the hell?" I said as I hurried across the street, spotting a pair of long legs flailing back and forth on the ground. As I got closer, I realized the person was stuck under the porch, which looked like it just caved in.

"Ma'am?" I said as I skidded to a stop beside the woman.

"I'm Officer Harlowe with the Sweet Water sheriff's department. Are you injured?"

"I'm stuck!" The voice was somewhat familiar with an irritated southern drawl that had me arching an eyebrow.

"All right, I'm here to help you," I said. "Do you have any weapons or sharp objects on you of any kind?"

"Not unless you count this blasted cat I'm holding!"

I bit back a laugh, shaking my head as I studied the array of wood tucked around her hips. Quickly and safely as possible, I shifted the fallen debris away until I could see her lower back. "I'm going to pull you out now," I said. "Do I have permission to touch your body?"

"No, please find another way to get me out of here," she snarked.

"Ma'am, I need your permission or I can't help you."

"For goodness' sake of course you have my permission, just please get me out of here before I'm eaten alive by bugs!"

I reached down, gripping her hips and hauling her backward until her body came free of the hole beneath the porch. A wiggling black cat struggled in her arms, but the woman held tight to the thing as she clambered to her feet. She didn't even bother looking at me, just examined the cat and then gently tugged at a jar that was apparently stuck over its head.

"There," she said. "Are you happy now?"

The thing immediately stopped struggling once it was free of the jar, instead curling up in her arm like it was exhausted from the battle.

"Sure, you just rest while I deal with this mess," she chided the cat.

A light breeze blew between us, and the strong scent of vodka hit my nose. "Ma'am, have you been drinking tonight?"

"No," she said, finally turning to face me.

"I'm going to need you to be honest—" I froze, my mouth parted open, my next line of questioning dying on my tongue.

16

"Anne," I whispered her name, my entire body reacting to the sight of her. Her long gold hair was mussed from being stuck under the dilapidated porch and had a few leaves sticking out of it, but her eyes were wide and blue and as beautiful as ever.

"*Jim*?" she asked, tilting her head like she didn't quite recognize me.

I guess I looked a bit different since high school—I had a full beard that I kept neat along my jaw, and had traded our school uniforms for my police one.

My brain caught up with my body, and I cleared my throat. "How much have you had to drink tonight?"

She gaped up at me, blinking a few times like she was in shock. "I haven't had a single drop."

I arched a brow at her, and she glanced down at her clothes, which were visibly wet.

"I promise," she said, shifting the sleeping cat in her arms. "I know it looks bad, but I swear I haven't had anything to drink."

"We got calls about an erratic driver—"

"Well, that's his fault," she cut me off, jarring the limp cat in her arms. "He ran out in front of me, and then I saw his head was stuck and I couldn't leave him like that."

I studied her for a few seconds. She definitely didn't appear inebriated. Her eyes were clear and her movements were controlled.

"Jim," she said, sighing. "Please. I can't...If my father gets wind of this, I'll be in so much trouble. I'm already in enough as it is."

I tilted my head, wondering what she meant by that but it wasn't exactly my place to ask now was it? It didn't stop incessant urge to help her with whatever trouble she was in. Didn't stop the flicker of anger at the mention of her father, either. That prick was the reason why Anne and I hadn't built a life together, one filled with passion and laughter and fights and making up and all the things we once lived for.

Fuck me. It'd been *years*...how could I still think that way?

I leaned down so our faces were only inches apart. It'd been a decade since I'd last seen her and she still felt just as tiny compared to my six-foot-four frame.

Her eyes flared at my sudden nearness, and I couldn't stop the heat streaking through my veins as they fluttered from my eyes to my lips and back again. Damn, did she think I was about to kiss her like no time had passed between us at all?

Shit, I wasn't exactly against the idea.

"Breathe for me," I finally said, remembering why the hell I was here in the first place. Two minutes with her and I was reduced to the need that had always been so intense between us.

"What?" she asked.

"Breathe on me," I said, eyebrows raised while I waited.

"No," she said, covering her mouth with her free hand. "What if I have bad breath? I haven't had a sip of water since I got off work—"

"You won't have bad breath," I said, barely biting back a laugh. "It's this or I have to run a full citation, including a breathalyzer."

"Oh," she said, dropping her hand. She rolled her eyes, then blew onto my face.

There wasn't a hint of alcohol on her breath. Good for her, she wasn't lying. Not that she'd ever been much of a liar. She always liked to speak the truth, even if it was hurtful. It was one of the things that made me fall for her years ago.

"Happy? That felt ridiculous." The cat in her arms shifted, and she shook her head.

"Yeah," I said. "You're free to go."

"Thank you so very much, Officer Harlowe," she said,

drawing out my title with a little attitude that sent me straight back to high school where I lived to rile her up.

Instinctively, I stepped toward her, plucking a leaf from her hair. She tipped her chin, holding my gaze, not once backing away from the closeness between us.

Were those chills sweeping across the bare skin of her neck?

Fire blazed beneath my skin like an electric charge, and it was strong enough that I took a giant step back.

"Small world," she said. "Running into you like this."

"Technically I got called to you."

"I'm not sad it was you who came to my rescue," she said. "Maybe we could grab coffee sometime. Catch up—"

"That's not a good idea," I cut her off.

I'd only seen her for a matter of minutes and I was already spiraling.

God, I missed her.

I'd never *stopped* missing her. But it'd been years. It was easier when the small-town gossip mill would report her continued travels anywhere but Sweet Water. Now that she was standing in front of me? It was all I could do to not reach for her, hold her, laugh with her like we used to.

"Right," she said, but I saw a flash of hurt in her eyes. "I'm sure you can handle this then." She gently shoved the cat into my arms, who tensed up at the change in hands.

"What do you expect me to do with him?" I called after her as she headed back to her car.

"I figure you know the best animal shelter in town, Officer Harlowe." She slammed her car door shut, heading off in the opposite direction before I could respond.

I looked down at the cat, and shook my head.

"Smooth, Jim," I said to myself. "Real fucking smooth."

* * *

19

After dropping the cat off at the shelter and finishing my shift, I changed into regular clothes and headed toward Main Street.

"You're late," Ridge grumbled the second I walked through his shop's door. The sign said closed, but he lived right above his tattoo parlor so he'd left it unlocked for me.

"Sorry," I said, following him up the stairs to his apartment. He immediately cracked open a couple beers, handing me one. "It was a weird night," I said after taking a sip.

"It's Sweet Water," he said. "How weird can it get?"

I tilted my head, taking another drink as we leaned on opposite sides of his kitchen counter. "Anne VanDoren weird."

Ridge nearly spit out his beer. "No shit?"

"No shit."

"Explain." Ridge motioned to me with the bottle in his hand, and we both took seats on the barstools around his kitchen island.

His loft was small, but functional, the walls decorated with art of his own making, much like his skin. He was covered in ink, and had even given me a couple of my tattoos, not only because he was my best friend, but because he was one of the best tattoo artists in the country. Even the freaking Carolina Reapers came to see him.

I took another drink before telling him what had happened with Anne, all to the furrowed brow, sullen look of my grumpy friend. I mean, he wasn't exactly an angry guy, he just constantly looked like it.

"She said she'd just got off work?" Ridge asked after I was finished.

"Yeah, I guess she did," I said, almost completely missing that detail. I'd been too busy being shocked at the sight of her. "Of all the times I've thought about seeing her again, I never thought I'd run into her like that." I laughed, and Ridge grunted.

"So she's back in town for a while then," he said, eying me.

"I guess. If she has a job."

"Where does she work?"

"I have no idea."

"And you're not going to try and find out?" he asked, setting his beer on the island.

"Why would I do that?"

"I don't know. Maybe because you moped about her for years and now she's back. It's not like you're seeing anyone."

He wasn't wrong. I'd dated off and on over the years, but all those relationships had been fleeting, and not one of them had ever really wanted it to be more serious, which had been fine with me.

"You're one to talk," I fired back. "Your longest relationships don't last past the night." I took another drink. "And I didn't *mope*."

"You did," he said matter-of-factly. "And I don't need a relationship period."

"Yeah, asshole Ridge doesn't need anyone at all," I said. "Present company excluded."

Ridge flipped me off, and I laughed.

"I've got no issue with how I live," he said, leaning closer over the island. "But ten bucks says you've got issue with not taking her up on that olive branch she tried to hand you."

I glared at him, but he wasn't wrong. I was already regretting shutting her down as quickly as I did. It was a knee-jerk reaction though—my heart's way of trying to protect itself. Because she'd wrecked it ten years ago and I'd never fully recovered.

Still, she may have only meant the offer as a friendly catch-up, not a date. For all I knew, she was married again. I'd seen the announcement sections enough to know she'd been married a few times. And it never hurt any less, even though it shouldn't.

Ten years man, get the fuck over it.

"Another ten says you don't go two days without tracking her down," Ridge said, smirking at me.

"You're on," I said, clinking his bottle with mine. "I have no desire to see her. I've been down that road before and it's a painful one."

Ridge looked at me skeptically but I just shrugged.

I needed it to be true.

I needed to stay away from her.

Because there was no world in which Anne VanDoren and me got our happily ever after.

CHAPTER 3

Anne

I softly closed the door behind me, practically tiptoeing out of my mother's room.

"How did that go?" Persephone asked me once I made it down the hall and to the den. I took a seat next to her on the leather sofa, nodding.

"Really well," I said, relief uncoiling some of the tension in my muscles. Mom was recovering in her master bedroom with every luxury at her fingertips. Hell, she even complained about being restless with all the down time and meds schedule, but she would never dare deviate from the doctor's instructions.

"That's wonderful," my sister said, reaching across the space between us to squeeze my hand.

It was an effort to not pull away from her, the reaction was so ingrained in me.

I took a deep breath and simply allowed myself to *feel*.

To feel comfort in her support, her love. To feel happy that Mom beamed at my three weeks' sober success. It was all so different for me—actually feeling the emotions that came with being sober, not to mention actually being on the receiving end of my mother's praise for once.

I loved making her proud, making my sister proud. I really did. I liked the accomplished feeling, even if I was only doing the bare minimum right now compared to what Persephone did in a regular day in her life—

Stop comparing.

Readjust.

I used the tools Dr. Casson had given me to realign my thought process when it came to my sister.

Persephone lives her life. I live mine. She does amazing things. I do amazing things.

The hard part about the process was finding worth in the events of my current life.

You didn't take a drink last night when you easily could've.

That much was true. The bottle had been right there acting like an escape route straight to numbville.

You saved that grumpy cat's life.

I laughed out loud at the thought, thinking that was a stretch. I'm sure the feral beast would've gotten the jar off somehow.

"What's so funny?" Persephone asked gently.

"Last night," I said, shaking my head. "It was eventful."

"Was *Lyla's Place* packed?"

"It's almost always packed," I answered. "Her food is really that good. But no, it was what happened after work."

After work.

I don't think I've ever uttered those words before in my life, and they filled me with the oddest little sensation—pride?

Maybe. I wasn't entirely sure what it felt like to be really proud of something.

"What happened?"

I relayed the events of last night to my sister, her NHL Carolina Reaper husband coming in midway through the story.

Cannon immediately took a seat on the armrest of the

couch, close enough to slide his hand lovingly down Persephone's back. The move was so effortless it almost looked like he wasn't even aware he was doing it. Those two were the real deal, something I'd grossly mistaken when I'd met Cannon weeks ago.

"And the officer just let you go?" Cannon asked, his tone in the usual deep tenor that bordered on this side of gruff. After getting to know him, I understood it wasn't personal, it was just his voice. He was like the scary big brother I never had.

"He did," I said, having left out the part about the officer being my ex-boyfriend. It was instinct to keep anything that mattered to me to myself, because the things I valued often had a way of getting tainted by my family, whether by their disapproval or their indifference.

But that was then.

This was now.

I shifted on my seat, focusing on my sister. "It was Jim."

Her lips parted, and Cannon's brow furrowed as he took in her shock.

"Who is Jim?" Cannon asked when Sephie seemed too stunned to speak.

"Oh, Anne," she said. "How was it seeing him again?"

"Hard," I admitted, my heart sighing a little at being able to be open and honest with my sister after so many years of strain between us. Thanks to therapy, it was getting easier for me to separate my trauma from my sister who had no hand in it, and moreso, didn't even *know* about it.

"I can't imagine," she said. "How did he look?" She raised her brows, practically starving for details.

"Really good." I laughed. "Too good. He's got this whole Jack Ryan thing going on now."

A warm shiver raced down the center of my body with the thought of last night. Jim was all man now, the only pieces of the teenager I'd known flickering in his green eyes. Carved muscles filled out his police officer's uniform, and the dark full beard over his strong jaw was a new kind of kryptonite I didn't know I had.

"Who the hell is Jim?" Cannon asked, his features full of curiosity that only made me laugh harder. Sephie told me the Reapers were just as gossipy as we were.

"He's an old friend of Anne's," Sephie explained.

"An old boyfriend?" Cannon asked.

Sephie looked to me, giving me the space to decide how much I let Cannon into my life. I loved her for it, especially since my family thrived on making decisions on my behalf without a single regard to my own desires.

"Yes," I answered Cannon.

"So that's why he let you go," he said, and Sephie lightly smacked his tatted arm. "What?" he asked. "There's no way any other cop would've let her just drive home when she was covered in alcohol."

"Cannon Price," Sephie chided.

"No, he's right," I said. "I was lucky." I shook my head. "And stupid."

"You weren't stupid," Sephie said, scooting closer to me. "You had a vulnerable moment. That's to be expected. Change doesn't happen overnight."

I studied her blue eyes that were so like my own, and there wasn't a hint of false support or judgment. She genuinely believed in me and wanted me to get better. God, I can't believe I'd let my own trauma get in the way of loving my sister in a healthy way for so many years.

That's in the past, which I can't change. I can only change how I feel in the present.

"Next time," she continued. "Call me. I don't care what time it is. If you're struggling, call me and I'll be there."

"Or me," Cannon said. "If I'm not at practice or a game, I'll be there too."

Tears bit the backs of my eyes, my heart swelling in my chest. I didn't deserve their kindness, especially after my behavior when I first met Cannon. I'd come on to him, for fuck's sake. Sure, I'd done it as a test under the ridiculous notion that I'd be saving Persephone from a failed marriage like I'd experienced so many times, but I was wrong.

So very wrong.

"Thank you," I managed to choke out before sucking in a breath. I didn't need to turn into a puddle right now. "I don't deserve you two—"

"Andromeda," my father's voice cut over my conversation, and I immediately sat up straighter. He had that tone, the one he so often used with me—a combination of disappointment and authority.

"Yes?" I asked as he came around the corner.

"A word."

That's all he said before turning on his heels and heading no doubt to his office. It was the source of his power after all, and I'd suffered many a lecture in there over the years.

"You don't have to go in there," Sephie said when I got up off the couch. "Or I can come with you."

I smiled softly at her. "If I really want to reconnect with this family in a healthy way, I have to not only fight my own battles but also listen and do my best to make our parents proud. Ignoring him won't do me any favors in that department, but thank you for offering."

She hugged me quickly. "I'm so proud of you," she said, and I tried not to squirm away from the gesture and the compliment. "We're heading out," Sephie said, her and Cannon following me out of the den. They interlocked hands, my sister almost melting into her new husband. It was super cute, if not a little disgusting. Who the hell was ever that happy? "Call me later?" she asked, and I nodded, waving goodbye as they left.

I stood outside of my father's office door for far longer than necessary. Finally, after telling myself I'd disappointed him in much greater ways, I pushed open the door.

He was a sight behind his desk, all power and age and wisdom as he motioned for me to sit in the chair across from him.

"I heard everything," he said as an intro, and I immediately slumped in my chair. I might as well be sixteen again, being scolded for sneaking out after curfew.

"I didn't drink," I said.

"I don't believe you."

Ouch. That smacked me right in the chest.

"Don't look at me like that," he continued. "It's hard to believe you when you've spent the last decade lying to me."

I furrowed my brow. "I rarely lied to you," I said. "I just never behaved like you wanted me to."

"You made false accusations against our security guard—someone who has been with us since you were little—a mere few weeks ago."

Shame slithered beneath my skin like an oily serpent hellbent on eating my soul. "I know," I said, barely holding back the tears building in my chest. Goddammit, being sober was hard. I felt every single ounce of pain, regret, shame, all of it. "And I apologized. Profusely. It was wrong. Evil even. I know that. And I'm sorry. I really am, but I can't change the past. I'm doing everything I can to change the present."

Something like pity flashed across his features, and I couldn't decide if that was better or worse than his disappointment.

"Fine," he said. "I *can* see the change in you, Andromeda," he continued. "And Sephie has done nothing but sing the praises of your success."

Of course, if my sister said it then he would listen.

"But I'm not going to change my mind about your inheritance until you really prove to me that you're going to take care of yourself. That you care about your own well-being."

"I've got a job," I said. "Just like you asked. I show up to every session with Dr. Casson. I see our physician every two weeks for drug and alcohol tests without complaint. I'm trying—"

"You were soaked in vodka while driving, Andromeda," he cut me off.

"I. Didn't. Take. A. Drink." I had to grind each word out or I would crumble. He was damning me even while I actively tried to do every single thing he requested.

"Fine. Maybe you didn't. But it was too close. You know what the doctors said. If you continue—"

"I'll die."

"And I don't want that."

I looked up at him from where I'd been studying my hands, and I hated that I couldn't tell if he really meant that or if he was just saying it for the sake of my mother and sister. My relationship with my father had always been strained, long before any trauma I accumulated in my past. Hell, even before he forbade me to see the love of my life.

"I want you to participate in some community service," he said, and I held in my groan. Not that I was opposed to community service but I was shuffling a crammed schedule as it was. "I've already spoken to a friend at the Sweet Water sheriff's station. You'll be doing some clerical work there. It will be good for you to work in a space where you can see what happens to people who throw away their lives."

"The sheriff's station?" I asked, my heart skipping a beat.

Would I see Jim there? Work with him?

No, surely not. Clerical work would be in an office and he

obviously patrolled the streets. Still, I couldn't stop the train of thought.

"Yes," he said. "Do you take issue with that?"

"No, sir," I said.

"Good," he continued, his features shifting to a softer, more hopeful kind of look. "I also have someone I want you to meet."

"Who?"

"Do you remember the Washbrooks?"

"Vaguely," I answered, stretching my memory back in time. There were countless connections we were forced to entertain over the years. Powerful families or business prospects.

"They're some of our oldest friends," he continued, and I bit my tongue to stop myself from saying *his* oldest friends. I'd been gone for a decade, saying goodbye to this town as I tried to outrun my demons while collecting new ones. Those families had nothing to do with me. "And their son has made a name for himself as an investor. Quite impressive, actually."

An image of a young boy doing his best to eat everything the caterer set out on a linen covered table flashed behind my eyes. He couldn't have been more than seven when we'd met.

"Brad?" I asked, finally plucking the name from the recess of my mind.

"Yes," he said, an impressed look flashing in his eyes. God, I'd remembered a name and he looked at me like I just announced my non-profit had produced record numbers for the quarter.

Not that I had a non-profit, that was Sephie's department.

Mine? I messed up. Made mistakes. That's what I was good at.

Not anymore. I have value. I have worth.

"I have a dinner reservation tonight," he continued. "You'll meet Brad there."

I raised my brows at the demand.

"Please," he added. "He's a good kid. I just want you to see what life could be like if you searched for...companionship in the right places."

I swallowed the knot in my throat. The right places being places *he* approved of, of course. He'd never, not once, approved of anyone I decided to spend my time with, starting with Jim. And sure, the other men in my life had been a series of emotional and sometimes physically abusive assholes, but not Jim.

Never Jim.

A surge of need swelled inside me, a craving for his jokes, his optimistic outlook on the world and the people in it, his touch.

Sweet heavens, it had been ten years since I'd spoken to the man and one encounter with him last night had me in literal knots.

I had to stop thinking about him. He'd always been too good for me.

"Okay," I said, suddenly leaping at the chance to end this conversation.

Maybe it would be good for me to meet someone else. Not that I was ready for a relationship, but my father didn't need to know that. He likely wanted me to fall in love with Brad and his considerable wealth, marry him, and be taken care of for the rest of my life. If I married a good, upstanding citizen my father deemed worthy, then I would no longer be his problem or his burden.

I couldn't give that to him, not before fully healing myself first. But, a date never hurt anyone. And maybe it would help me stop thinking about the man I'd left behind when I ran away from this town.

"Wonderful," he said, and genuinely sounded happy. "I'll send you the details."

I nodded, and left the office with as much grace as I could muster.

* * *

"This is some place your father selected," Brad said from where he sat across from me at the table.

We'd just ordered appetizers and we were doing the *break the ice* dance while sipping on soda waters.

"It's nice," I said. "But if I'm being honest, I'd be more comfortable back at *Lyla's Place*."

Brad chuckled, an effortless smile lighting up his blue-gray eyes. He was beyond handsome, with various shades of dark blond hair that was styled to perfection, his frame muscled but more on the lithe side which fit how tall he was. The navy suit he wore only complemented his eyes, but it was the smile that likely drew everyone in—it was genuine, kind, and this side of mysterious.

All that and not a *single* flutter in my stomach.

Jim had barely touched me and I'd melted, and just the thought of him had my heart speeding up.

You have to stop thinking about him.

Right.

"I love *Lyla's Place*," Brad said as the waitress set down our calamari. "Best food in a hundred-mile radius if you ask me," he continued, then waved an arm to indicate the room we were in. "No offense to this place."

I laughed at that, taking a bite. "I work there."

"No way," he said, that smile widening. "Do you get to eat for free?"

Another laugh flew past my lips. He was certainly surprising. If I'd told any of my old "friends" that I was serving tables they would've turned up their noses at me right before disowning me as a friend completely.

"One meal per shift," I said, and Brad leaned back in his chair, shock coloring his chiseled features.

"Now I want a job there," he said. "How long have you been working there?"

"Three whole weeks," I said, very proud of myself.

"Do you love it?"

"I actually do," I admitted. "I've never served tables before and I find it's really...satisfying."

Brad nodded, munching on the appetizer before taking another sip of his soda water. When we were first seated, I explained to him it wouldn't bother me if he ordered a drink, but he insisted on ordering what I did. It was sweet, and he was definitely shooting off all kinds of green flags, but we were missing that initial spark of chemistry.

"That's wonderful," he said. "Doing what you love is what life is all about."

I grinned at that, and then decided Brad was way too nice a guy to give the wrong impression to. When my father set up this date, I fully expected him to be the same kind of *I'm-better-than-everyone* type I'd dealt with countless times in the past. We'd only been chatting for a half hour and I could tell he was nothing like that.

"Can I be honest with you, Brad?" I asked, nerves tangling in my stomach. There was every chance he would get offended by my truth or he could tell my father off for setting us up in the first place, but I couldn't lead him on.

"I would prefer it," he said.

"I know my father connected us because he has high hopes of us forming a relationship," I said. "But I'm in not in a place in my life that I can have one. And even if I was..."

"It's not here," he said, motioning between us. "The zing."

"It's not." I laughed again, and he joined in. "But that has nothing to do with you. You're handsome and smart..."

"Don't stop there," he said, grinning.

"And funny," I finished. "I don't want you to think it has anything to do with you."

"I like you too," he said, raising his glass to mine. I clinked it and we both took a sip. "In that way too awesome people can like each other without anything else involved."

I smiled, half expecting a wave of awkwardness to wash over the table and send us packing, but it never came.

"So now that *that's* out of the way," he said after the waitress set our entrées in front of us. "We can be friends."

"Really?" I practically blurted out the question.

"Really," he said, cutting into his steak. "I like you, even if we aren't destined to be wed and join our great families," he said in a mock-regal voice. "Since we're being honest," he continued. "The last thing I want is a betrothal right now or a relationship, but my parents keep trying. Relentlessly. It's like they're worried I won't give them an heir or something as if we're in Victorian era England." He shook his head. "I'm quite happy with my life and I'm not looking for it to change any time soon."

Relief crashed through me.

"But I'd love to be friends," he continued. "Especially someone who understands what it's like to not be the exact version of what they're parents want."

"I can't remember the last time I had an actual friend," I admitted, even though images of Jim flashed through my mind. He was my friend first, but it had always felt more than that with him. More intense, more joyful, more everything.

"That makes me sad," he said, his bright smile falling to a frown.

"I'm all right—"

"Not for you," he cut me off. "For the people who missed out on your company."

I laughed and shook my head. "You barely know me."

"I'm a people reader." Brad shrugged. "It doesn't take me long to figure someone out."

"Oh really?"

He nodded, taking another bite of steak. "That and anyone who bypass caviar and lobster, racing straight to the dessert table is good in my book."

"You remember that?" I tried not to look embarrassed at the childhood memory.

"Sure do," he said. "Those parties were so boring, weren't they? I would never force my kids to go to those things, or if I had to, I would at least set up something cool and entertaining for them while the adults did business."

"Right?" I asked, settling into an easy dinner now that the pressure was totally off.

Honesty wasn't that bad after all. And after everything, I could really use a friend.

Brad raised his glass again, holding it toward mine. "To not doing what our parents expect us to do."

I laughed, clinking his glass. "I couldn't agree more."

CHAPTER 4

Jim

I added two sugars to the dark roast in my favorite mug, then strolled back to my desk. Today would be my first day of training our newest recruits with a special intro-duction to all things Sweet Water and how our department operated, and while I was excited for the new gig, I had those first-day-of-school jitters...God help me if anyone realized it.

Taking a good sip of coffee helped soothe away the nerves I knew were unnecessary. I was a good cop, and that's why my superior selected me for this task. The newest hires had already completed their required academy training, and this would act as a transition course into our department. I'd miss patrolling and answering calls, but it was only six weeks. I could handle anything for six weeks.

"How's your morning, Harlowe?" Tanner asked as he got settled at his desk.

"Going good," I said before glancing at my watch. "Would be even better if my volunteer showed up."

Volunteers were hard to come by, and this one was already five minutes late—if they didn't show up I'd be handling the full brunt of the program which was built to be ran by two.

We couldn't afford to pull another officer from our small department to help me, so we had to depend on free help.

"I'm sure they'll show up soon," Tanner encouraged me by raising his mug in the air and we did an air cheers before I headed to the back of the station where we'd set up our designated training area.

The first four weeks of would focus on Sweet Water politics, laws, and special interests, which meant we'd be spending all our time in the conference room going over tons of paperwork, histories, and the like. The last two weeks I'd assign each new hire to a partner for patrolling, giving us all a break from the school-like situation. But until that time came, I really needed help gathering all the course materials and then inputting responses and grades for the tests. Could I do it all on my own? Absolutely. Did I want to? Not really.

"This is where you'll be working." Tanner's voice sounded just outside the door to the conference room, and I turned just in time to see *Anne* walk through the door after him.

Fucking hell, she looked divine in a pair of black pants that hugged her long legs, tapering off at the ankles right above a pair of black stilettos that clicked against the tile as she walked inside. She wore a royal blue blouse that climbed up her delicate neck, making her blue eyes practically glow. Her long golden hair hung over her shoulders in waves, and those full, luscious lips turned up in the most adorable little surprised smile.

I had to focus extremely hard on not falling to my knees, she was *that* breathtaking.

"Officer Harlowe is heading up the program," Tanner continued. "He'll let you know what you need to do." Tanner tilted his head at me. "Harlowe?" he asked. "You good?"

I cleared my throat, blinking out of the stupor Anne's sudden appearance put me in. "Yes," I said. He nodded and headed out, leaving us alone in the room.

Was it hot in here? I tugged at my uniform shirt, desperately needing some air.

"Sorry I'm late," she said, striding over to the small desk in the back corner of the room. She set down her bag, then turned to lean against the desk. "I couldn't decide what to wear."

My lips parted, a response totally tangled in my throat.

Fuck man, speak.

"I mean, what does one wear to a forced volunteer program?" her voice was all tease, and I cocked an eyebrow at her. She shrugged. "I highly doubt my father knew I'd be working directly under you when he pulled strings to get me in here."

The mention of her father shifted everything inside me, transforming me into the pissed off teenager that wanted nothing more than to run away with the girl I'd been forbidden to see. I took a step closer to her, unable to keep the distance between us.

"From what I recall," I said, my voice low. "You never minded working beneath me before."

Her lips parted, a small gasp rushing from them. I tracked the reaction, satisfaction rolling through me right before reality slapped me across the face.

I was at work and that comment was incredibly inappropriate. I opened my mouth to apologize, but she smiled up at me, her eyes shining with something close to joy.

"I missed that mouth of yours," she fired right back, never one to miss a beat.

Fuck, this woman could hit all of my buttons with just a handful of words. Hell, she didn't need words, she could bring me to my knees with a simple look. It didn't matter that ten years had passed since we'd been together, it didn't matter that we'd never gone all the way in our relationship—one look at her and she still felt like *mine*.

But she wasn't.

She wasn't anything more than my volunteer.

"You'll be working over here," I said, clearing my throat like it would help clear my head. I needed to get a fucking grip. I wasn't a love-starved teenager anymore, I was a grown ass man.

"Cute," she said as I motioned to the desk behind her. She walked around it and took a seat. "What exactly do you need me to do, James?"

The way she said my name had lightning streaking through my veins. She only ever called me that when she wanted to get a rise out of me. I was Jim through and through and would never be the formal *James* her family wanted me to be. Not that any of that mattered anymore.

"I've written down a list of tasks here," I said, handing her the notebook I'd prepped last night while watching the Reaper game.

She took the list and quickly read over it. I didn't bother asking her if she could handle it, I knew she could. After a few seconds, she glanced up at me. "How long is this program again?"

"Six weeks."

She visibly swallowed, her eyes churning with something I couldn't quite place.

"Is that okay with you?" she asked. "Working with me for that long?"

Her question made the reality of the situation sink in.

I'd see her every single day. Work with her. Listen to her. Smell that delightful perfume she'd always worn, the floral and spicy scent hitting me as we spoke.

Fuck me.

"Yes," I finally managed to say. "As long as you're comfortable with it?"

She smiled, coming around the desk, stopping so close I

could've reached down and captured that grin between my lips if I wanted to.

Which I didn't...*couldn't* want that.

"If you are, I am," she said.

"Good," I said, then just stood there staring down at her because I could. She didn't squirm under my gaze, didn't try to back away. She met my eyes with the unabashed strength that had always drawn me to her in the past. She'd changed a little, but she was still the same in so many ways.

"Jim," she said, her lips poised on the tip of a question.

"Officer Harlowe," a female voice said from the doorway, stopping whatever Anne had been about to say. I took a casual step away from Anne, facing one of the new hires. "Is there anywhere in particular we need to sit?"

I shook my head, gesturing to the tables in the room. "Sit wherever you'd like."

Another four new hires filed in behind the first one, all spreading out throughout the room since it wasn't packed. Sweet Water was a small town, so it wasn't like we'd hired twenty or more officers like some bigger cities did.

Either way, the room felt about ten times smaller with Anne directly behind me. Her presence filled the room in a way nothing else ever did, and I swear I could feel her gaze on my skin as I started the first lecture.

After a full day, separated only by a small lunch break, we finally reached the end of the first class.

"That was impressive," Anne said after the new hires had left the room.

I blew out a breath. "You think?"

"Absolutely," she said, hooking her bag over her shoulder. "You had them captivated."

I smiled, pride swelling in my chest the way it always did whenever she complimented me. Damn, my body responded to her in exactly the same way as it had ten years ago, how was that possible?

"You did great too," I said, giving her credit where it was due. "We would've lost two hours if you hadn't saved the day with the tech-savviness."

She laughed, equal parts warm and wild and fuck me it was one of the best sounds in the world. I wanted to kiss that smile, wanted to drag other sounds from her lips like moans and whimpers and listen to her say my name in that breathy, blissful way only she was capable of.

"I've managed to keep up on the trends," she said. "New software and apps have always been easy for me to figure out."

Thankfully too, because I didn't have a clue when it came to the presentation app I had to show to the new hires earlier.

"Well," she said, glancing around the empty room. "Have a good night." She headed toward the door.

Have a good night.

See you tomorrow.

Take it easy.

"Are you hungry?"

That's what came out of my mouth instead of any of the other appropriate responses.

She turned around, surprise flashing over her features. "Starved."

Well, that settled that.

"Let me change, then we'll head out."

She stopped me in the doorway, her hand on my chest. "I thought you said this was a bad idea?"

I said that two nights ago when she invited me for coffee, but that was before I saw her again today. Before I spent an entire day with her, trapped in a room and feeling more alive than I had in years just from being around her.

"It is a bad idea," I said, and she dropped her hand, her eyes falling to study her stilettos. I tipped her chin up, cursing myself for the contact but relishing it all the same. "But don't we always have fun doing bad things?"

Her lips parted, and I had to physically stop myself from dragging my thumb over her bottom lip. I managed to head past her, hurrying to change, and had us at a two-top table at *Lyla's Place* within fifteen minutes.

The silence between us wasn't unbearable, but there was a tension to it that made me ache.

"Anne," Lyla, the owner of the best restaurant in town, said as she walked past our table. "Aren't you in here enough?" she asked. "What brings you in on your night off?"

I snapped my head to Anne, shock radiating all over me. She worked here? When she said she had a job, I figured it was at one of her father's many corporations or connections.

"This is the best place to eat in town," Anne said.

Lyla smiled at her but shook her head. "I'll cook up something special for you two."

"Thanks," Anne called to Lyla's back, which was covered in a white chef's jacket as she hurried back to the kitchen.

The restaurant was half full, with more people coming in by the minute.

"I didn't know you worked here," I said after the waitress brought our iced teas.

"You didn't ask," she said.

Fair.

"Speaking of things we didn't ask," she continued. "Are you married?"

I cocked an eyebrow at her. "Do you think I'd be here with you if I was?"

Heat churned in her eyes. "No," she said. "But this isn't a date, is it?"

"You said you were hungry," I said instead of addressing the question. I didn't know what this was other than me being incapable of staying away from her now that she was back in town.

She pursed her lips. "So you're not in a relationship?"

"No," I said, shaking my head.

The smile she wore did something to me, making me shift in my chair with a sense of pride and need that was hard to contain.

"How long have you been a cop?"

"Eight years now," I said, sighing at the easier shift in conversation. "I went to the academy right after high school."

"It suits you," she said, and I grinned.

"I think so," I said, shrugging. "I love my job. Love helping the community I grew up in." She nodded, and I pressed on. "What about you. What did you get up to right after high school?"

She huffed out a laugh. "Like you don't already know," she said, scanning the room. "Everyone in Sweet Water has been privy to the life I've lived."

"They may know what the social sites reported on, but they don't know the truth."

"And you want to know the truth?"

"Always," I said. "You know that."

She worried her bottom lip between her teeth, and I couldn't help but track the move. There would be no pushing her, I knew that and I never would, so I waited, patient and tuned in on whatever she wanted to give me.

"The truth is...nothing," she finally said. "I've done abso- lutely nothing of note in the last ten years." She shook her head. "You went to the academy and forged a life for yourself, and I lost myself while traveling and leaving a string of mistakes behind in my wake."

"I don't buy that," I said. She gaped at me. "I buy the travel part, but not the nothing part. Whatever your past is, it brought you to where you are now, so it's not nothing."

"Yes, where I am now. Having dinner with my ex who is now kind of my boss in between waiting tables, living in a studio apartment, and practically dancing through hoops to satisfy my family's requirements to be accepted into the family again." She slapped a hand over her mouth, her eyes widening with shock like she didn't mean to say any of that out loud. "I'm sorry," she said. "That was an uncalled-for outburst."

"That wasn't an outburst," I said leaning closer over the table. "That's called venting, and I'm here for it."

"I've never been able to hold back with you, have I?" she asked, nothing but raw, open vulnerability in her eyes.

I shook my head. "Never been a need to."

"Thanks, Jim," she said, sighing.

"For what?"

"For the other night," she said then shrugged. "For back then. For now. All of it."

I swallowed around the sudden tension in my throat. Our waitress chose the perfect time to bring us our meals, saving me from opening my mouth to say something I'd regret—like how happy I was to see her or how much I enjoyed talking to her or how much I'd missed her.

None of those things would do either of us any good. If I knew anything, I knew that we may be older, but nothing had changed. Our circumstances were still the same—she was a VanDoren and I was a Harlowe. She was social royalty and I was blue collar all the way. And as much as I might've wished it, she was very clearly still doing whatever it took to appease her parents' sometimes impossible expectations.

"I have no recollection of that," Anne said after we finished dinner and lingered outside of the restaurant. Night had fully taken over, leaving the quiet space covered in a dark indigo with only the glow surrounding Lyla's sign illuminating the area around us.

"Seriously?" I laughed. "You don't remember talking me

into stealing the headmaster's car and parking it on the football field?

"Not an inkling," she teased, but there was laughter in her eyes.

"I suppose you don't remember me kissing you senseless for an hour after that either?" The question was out of my mouth before I could stop it, the memory playing out in full force in my mind.

"Senseless?" she asked. "I don't recall you being that good of a kisser to make me *senseless* enough to let you steal a car. You were a soon-to-be police officer for heaven's sake!"

I narrowed my gaze on her. "Don't you dare," I teased. "You know I'm a phenomenal kisser."

"If I can't remember then how good could you really be?" she fired right back.

The blood turned hot in my veins, my head spinning from the game we played. The night had been perfection—laughing and reminiscing over amazing food. It was like no time had passed at all.

"Maybe I should remind you." I stepped closer, and she retreated until her spine pressed against the building, the shadows of the night coating us in near darkness.

"You think so?" she asked, her voice slightly breathless.

"All you have to do is say the word," I said, my pulse skyrocketing. This was a dangerous game, but I fucking lived for it.

A wild smile shaped her lips. "Remind me."

My mouth was on hers in an instant, spanning the distance between us until nothing separated us but clothes. I shifted my thigh between her legs, cupping her face in my hands. Her lips were soft and insistent as we crashed together, a decade's worth of tension unraveling and ramping up again in the span of a breath.

Fuck, she felt good against me, all smooth curves and

warmth. I tipped her head back, and she parted for me, letting me sweep my tongue inside her mouth, claiming her, exploring her, relearning what made her arch against me and what made her gasp. She fisted my shirt, drawing me closer as she kissed me back, giving and taking, taking and giving.

This was fire.

This was joy.

This was my girl.

The one who made me fall and never recover. The one who taught me to live and take risks and chase my dreams. The one who was easy to laugh with, the one who was easy to love.

Love? Fuck no, I wasn't going down that road.

But this? I could do this all damn night. She wanted to push me, challenge me, have me help her remember what it was like between us?

I'd do my best to make sure she never forgot me again.

CHAPTER 5

Anne

J im's kiss was just as good as I remembered it.

Dominate and compassionate.

Claiming and consuming.

I gripped his shirt, clinging to him, my mind whirling as he curled his tongue against the roof of my mouth. Warm chills burst across my skin, heat coiling tight in my core. He slid one hand from my cheek over my neck and around to the back of it, holding me there as he licked into my mouth, a perfect demonstration of what he'd do if he ever got between my legs. My entire body went tight and loose at the thought, at the *surrender* in the idea.

I wanted more.

I wanted *him*.

I kissed him back hungrily, giving him everything in return. What started off as a fun game was quickly turning into a frenzy I didn't know how to stop, and I wasn't entirely sure I wanted to.

His other hand dropped, wrapping around my lower back and urging me closer, the motion dragging me against his massive thigh tucked between my legs. The friction made a tiny whimper escape my lips, and he pulled back, looking at me, his eyes flaring.

"Make that sound again," he demanded, repeating the move only with a little more force this time.

I couldn't stop the half-gasp, half-moan that escaped my lips, and I barely had a chance to think before his mouth was on me again, almost like he wanted to devour the sound. My heart beat wildly against my chest, crying out with a need for *more, more, more*.

"*James*," I said against his lips, remember how crazy it drove him when I called him that during our make-out sessions of the past.

But this was now, and we no longer had the constraints we did then. I was desperate for him, starved for him. I wanted to go to his place or mine or anywhere we could keep going. I never wanted this to end.

He drew back again, his lips parting—

"Jim?" a male voice called from just outside the restaurant's door which was a few feet away. "That you over there? What are you doing?"

Jim took a step away from me, putting enough distance between us that a cold rush of air washed over my overheated skin.

"Ridge," Jim said, clearing his throat when the man came into view.

He looked like a bounty hunter come to collect our souls. Okay, maybe that was a bit over dramatic but the guy was tall, muscled, covered in tats, and glaring at me like I was the damn devil.

"What are you doing here?" Jim asked, trying like hell to sound casual...but why? Was he embarrassed about kissing me? I mean, sure, we probably shouldn't have lost control in public like that but we were adults.

"Food," Ridge grumbled, jerking a thumb toward the restaurant door. "What are you doing?" he asked again.

"Just dinner," he said, almost like he was trying to assure his friend nothing else was going on.

Rejection and embarrassment flooded my body, threatening to have me curl in on myself.

How silly of me to think he felt what I did in that kiss. He really was just playing a game, one *I* started, and now he was practically holding his hands up for his friend like he was ashamed of being caught with me.

Well, I'd had enough of that shit in my life. More times than I could count. I just never thought it would be from him. Especially after how amazing the night had been.

I shook my head. "Thanks for *dinner*," I said to Jim in the best, sweetest southern drawl I could muster. I didn't bother addressing his friend because he hadn't decided I was important enough to introduce.

Okay, it had only been a few seconds but damn it my emotions were all over the place. I'd gone from losing myself in the hottest kiss ever to feeling ashamed, like I'd done something wrong. And I was so over that. I was actually doing really damn well in my life right now, despite everything, and the last thing I needed was to feel like someone's mistake.

Especially Jim's.

"Anne," he called after me, but I waved him off, the tears already building behind my eyes as I hurried into my car.

God, times like this was when I'd reach for a drink to help soothe the embarrassment I made of myself.

But I couldn't do that anymore, couldn't hide from my emotions. I had to work through them if I wanted any kind of healthy growth, according to Dr. Casson.

I made it home in record time, my hand hovering over Sephie's number in my phone. Ultimately, I chucked my phone and climbed into bed. I couldn't be dependent on anyone or anything else anymore. I had to face reality.

I just hated that that reality included the ex-love of my life being ashamed of me.

"You know I can work with your schedule and give you more time off now that you're doing the community service," Lyla said as we prepped for the dinner rush. I'd had to duck out of community service an hour early today to make this shift, but Jim didn't mind.

In fact, Jim had been infuriatingly fine today. Not even a hint of regret or need or anything indicating the kiss had affected him at all.

I guess that was fair though. I mean, what had I really expected? I started a game and he finished it. End of story. I needed to take accountability for that and not hold it against him. It wasn't his fault it meant more to me than it did to him.

Dr. Casson would be so proud of me.

"That's all right," I answered her while rolling up flatware into napkins with magnolias printed on them.

Lyla's personality was as bubbly as her style, which consisted of lots of tasteful floral designs mixed with a modern edge throughout her restaurant. Whenever I did see her out of her chef's jacket, she leaned toward bright colors and fun prints, and I wasn't sure that I ever saw her without a smile on her face.

"You know how much I love working here," I continued. "And I'm so grateful you offered me a job when I came crawling in here." Almost literally. That first week of sobriety was a real bitch, but I was nothing if not determined. Not wanting to die will do that to you.

Lyla waved me off. "You're too sweet," she said, and I had to stop myself from shaking my head at her.

Sweet was the last word I'd use to describe myself. Lyla was sweet down to her core not only being genuinely nice but also by serving the community. She gave meals to people in need without blinking twice and always made sure she didn't waste a single scrap of food after the night wrapped up.

Jim was sweet, always asking if I needed coffee or water when he went to grab himself some, or holding my door open for me.

Me? I was spicy. Not in the cute fun way sometimes used to describe people, but in the literal sense that some people found me downright intolerable and at the very least I made some people uncomfortable. And I was fine with that because there were some people, few and far between, but some people who could handle my level of heat...or baggage or trauma or whatever label we wanted to slap on it. I'd ask the doc for clarification at our next session.

"All done," I said, showing off my hard work with a Vanna White display that made Lyla laugh.

She wrapped up her dark brown hair in a bun before heading to the sink to wash her hands. "Great job, love," she said. "Now get out there and sell my special." She winked at me.

I headed out of the kitchen backward, clenching my eyes shut. "A pan-seared Chilean sea bass with a cauliflower mash and roasted corn cakes?"

"That's the one," she said, grinning at me. "You've got this."

I blew out a breath and headed out of the kitchen and into the dining room, greeting the few other servers as I headed to my section.

I never expected to be so welcomed when I came begging for a job, but Lyla had pretty much made me realize that not everyone in Sweet Water cared about what the gossip columns wrote about my past. She treated me like she treated just about everyone else, with a fierce sort of kindness I'd never truly understand. I mean the *patience* that woman had. It was a marvel. A burner on her stove had blown out last week, severely reducing her work flow, and she'd barely uttered so much as a curse. I kind of wanted to be her when I grew up.

The dinner rush hit with a delightful chaos that I thrived in. I didn't have a second to stop and think or catch my breath, which I loved. No time to think meant no time to agonize if I was doing good enough or if I'd ever reach a moment in time where I didn't have to *question* if I was doing good enough.

"Anne," a familiar voice sounded behind me after I finished refilling one of my table's waters.

I spun around with a smile on my face.

"Brad," I said. "What brings you in here tonight?"

Our hostess settled him at a two-top table in my section, heading off to wait on the next customers. "I was in the neighborhood, so I thought I'd swing by and grab something to eat."

"Don't lie," I teased. "You came in here to see if I'd give you free food."

"I would never," he said, holding his hand over his heart. Dressed in a simple pair of slacks and a blue button-down, he looked no less done up than he had in his ten-thousand-dollar suit. Still, there was this sense of relatability and trustworthiness to him that made me genuinely happy to see him. "I came here to eat and chat with a friend."

I looked around, wondering where his friend was, and he laughed, drawing my attention back to him by gently grabbing my hand. "You," he said, shaking his head.

"Oh," I said, laughing at how ridiculous I must've looked.

"Damn," he said, releasing me. "You weren't joking about not having a real friend in a long time."

"I told you I'd be honest," I said. "No matter how sad it was."

"Not sad," he said. "Just..."

"Sad," I said, and we both laughed again. "Want me to order for you?" I asked, leaning down and lowering my voice. "I happen to know the chef."

"Please do," he said.

I patted his shoulder and spun around, ready to put the special in as his order, only to be stopped in my tracks by a very surly looking Jim in full uniform.

"Whoa," I said, hurrying over to him where he lingered by the hostess station. The muscle in his jaw tensed, his full beard doing nothing to hide it and everything to make him look even more intimidating as his eyes locked somewhere behind me. I followed his gaze, noting he was staring at Brad. "Is there an emergency, Officer Harlowe?" I asked.

He blinked a few times, focusing on me. "No," he grumbled. "I'm picking up food for Ridge. Guys' night."

"Oh, that sounds fun," I said, noting he kept glaring behind me.

"Who was that you were laughing with?" he asked, and I arched a brow at him.

"That's Brad," I answered. "He's a friend." Wow. That felt incredibly good to say. He wasn't an acquaintance or a connection or a fake-ass friend who only wanted to be with me because of my parent's money.

"He was holding your hand."

"He was not!" I chided him, shaking my head. "Not like that, anyway. It was a friendly gesture. Honestly, you sound jealous." But that couldn't be right, because he's the one who acted like our kiss didn't mean anything all day.

"Of a suit?" he asked, a playfulness returning to his eyes as he focused on me again. The hostess brought up his to-go order and he gathered it. "Not a chance."

My lips parted, but he spun around and headed out without another word.

Well, then. That was fine. That was fair.

But *damn*, if we kept up this hot and cold back-and-forth, it was going to be a long six weeks.

CHAPTER 6

Jim

I stared at the picture frames I had on my desk, the only two I had, and allowed myself sit with a heavy heart. One was of my mom, who I lost a few years ago. One was of my dad, who I lost when I was a kid.

Normally I could work with them looking at me and not feel the slightest hint of sadness, but it was always harder when Thanksgiving was close. It was the one holiday my mother cherished, the one she loved more than Christmas, and each one without her was tough.

"Training went well today," Anne said, jostling me out of my memories.

I shifted in my seat, nodding as I shut down my computer. "They're doing good."

"You're a good teacher," she said, stacking some papers in a pile and setting them on my desk. "These are all graded and inputted into the system like you asked."

"Thanks," I said, giving her a smile. We'd been working together for a week straight now and we'd fallen into this incredibly normal rhythm of being around each other. She'd never brought up the kiss, so I kept my mouth shut about it too. I'm sure she regretted it or maybe she didn't think it was a big deal since it had happened because we traveled a little too far down memory lane.

Either way, I couldn't help it, I loved seeing her every day. Even if it was just a friendship rekindling between us, it brought a certain sense of wholeness to my life that I didn't realize I was missing.

"Is there anything else you need?" she asked as I scooted back from the desk and tucked the chair under it.

The memory of her lips on mine, her body pliant beneath my hands swarmed my vision and filled my head so much I could barely breathe around it. I needed more of that, more of *her*.

"No," I said instead of voicing the truth. "That's all. I'll see you after Thanksgiving."

She nodded, heading back to the training room to collect her bag, I assumed.

"You're in so much trouble," Ridge's voice sounded from behind me, and I spun around from where I'd been staring after Anne to find him standing there with his arms folded over his chest.

"Who says?"

"That look on your face says."

I rolled my eyes. "Where are we going tonight?"

"Pasta."

"Cool."

"Have you decided if you're coming over tomorrow or not?" Ridge asked.

"I don't know..."

"Come on, a Blackstone Thanksgiving. You loved it last year."

"I know, I just—"

"You don't have plans for Thanksgiving?" Anne cut over me as she came back into the room, her purse in her hands.

Ridge glared at her. "Dinner with me *is* a plan."

Her eyes fluttered downward, and I wanted to punch Ridge. He had a grudge against her since he met me shortly after we'd broken up, but that was years ago. Couldn't he drop the overprotectiveness for five minutes?

"Right," she said. "Sorry, I just..." She straightened her spine, a breath restoring her usual confident exterior. "If you two would like to come to my house for Thanksgiving, we'd be more than happy to host you. We'll have plenty—"

"I'd rather get my balls tattooed in front of an audience than spend an entire evening with a house full of people whose only concern is who has more offshore accounts than the other."

"Jesus, Ridge," I chided. "Lay off it, will you?"

Anne laughed, and my eyes widened at how delightful and genuine it sounded. She was within rights to be in tears over Ridge's asshole comment, but she was laughing. "You sound like my brother-in-law," she said, swiping beneath her eyes.

"*Him* I like," Ridge grumbled.

"That's right," she said. "You did Cannon's most recent tattoo didn't you? The one with Persephone's name? *Not* on his balls of course," she added. "Not that I know of anyway."

Ridge grunted in response.

"The details of the pomegranate seeds were amazing. Seriously, you're a fantastic artist."

I cocked a brow at Ridge, who shifted on his feet.

"Thanks," he said, but no less gruffly.

"Anyway," she said. "The invitation stands. If either of you want to come." Her eyes met mine, and I swear I felt an electric charge the second we connected. It's like my heart jolted every time she looked at me like that, but she blinked, smiled at me, and headed out the door before I could say anything back.

"Fucking hell, man," Ridge groaned.

"What?"

"Trouble," he said. "So. Much. Trouble."

"Relax," I said, following him out. "I'm fine."

"I hope so, man," he said. "You were in a bad state when we met, and every road led back to her. I don't want to see you go through that shit again."

"That was years ago," I said. "It's not like that between us."

"Sure, and that's why you owe me twenty bucks, right? Because it wasn't two days before you tracked her down."

"Technically, she found me when she volunteered here."

He cocked a brow at me, but dropped it. "Well, if anything, there will be more for me tomorrow."

"What?"

"There's no way in hell you're coming to my Thanksgiving when you have an open invitation to hers."

I opened my mouth to argue, to tell him he was wrong, but closed it and shook my head. "You don't know me."

* * *

"This was a bad fucking idea," I grumbled to myself as the security guard waved me in as the gates to the VanDoren estate slowly opened.

I pulled through them, driving up the winding path toward the multi-million-dollar house, and I was sixteen again —awestruck and intimidated as hell. Back then I'd been an optimistic and hopeful teenager in love, never once thinking our differences in upbringing would come between us because Anne had never *treated* me differently.

It wasn't until she introduced me to her family—in this very house—that I realized we were doomed from the start.

That was the beginning of the end, no matter how hard I tried to fight it.

"That was rough," I said as we walked the grounds of Anne's estate. The lush greens seemed to go on forever, but I'd rather get lost in these trees than deal with her father another second.

Her mother was awesome, her little sister too, but her dad? I'd never been hated before, and I wasn't sure if he actually hated me or just disliked me, but it sure as hell wasn't good either way.

"I'm so sorry," she said, angry tears lining her eyes as she stopped to lean against a tree. "My dad is such a jerk sometimes."

I couldn't argue with her even though every instinct in me roared out to. A good boyfriend would say her parents were wonderful and that they'd come around. After tonight's dinner? I knew that would never happen. Not after her father had pulled me aside and practically bribed me to stay away from Anne. Told me that I was wasting her time with a relationship that would never amount to anything.

I mean, damn. I wasn't buying rings or anything but I did love her. How could he not see that?

I guess it was easy when he looked at me and all he saw was poor.

Two tears rolled down her cheeks. "Hey," I said, swiping them away with my thumbs. "It's okay. I'm not taking it personally—"

"How could you not take it personally? He was atrocious."

I laughed, unable to stop the smile on my lips with how adorable she looked when she was mad. "It doesn't bother me because it has nothing to do with us, right?"

I had to believe that. Needed to believe that. Just because her father didn't like me didn't mean things couldn't stay the same between us. Her mom liked me, and maybe I would earn her father's trust over time.

"Right," she said, but there was a wariness in her eyes.

"Anne," I said, forcing her to look at me. "The stuff he said in there, all the holier than thou stuff? It doesn't touch you."

She sighed, more tears falling as she reached up on her tiptoes and kissed me. Hard and fast enough to shift my thoughts completely. I held her against me, relishing her kiss, her touch, all thoughts and doubts forgotten.

I loved her.

She loved me.

That's all that mattered in the end.

The memory left a sour taste in my mouth as I handed my keys over to the valet stationed outside the entrance of the VanDoren home.

It had mattered, in the end. Not that I blamed Anne. Not entirely. Her father had forced an impossible decision on her and she reacted the only way she knew how. We ended our relationship, knowing the battle with her father would be exhausting. I had just hoped we could've lived fighting it together, but that never happened.

I clutched the bright pink box painted with white magnolias in my hands, doing my best not to crush the pumpkin pie inside as I climbed the steps. I stopped on the last step, lingering on the massive porch while I tried my best to shove the horrible memory from my mind. It'd been a decade, surely her father couldn't hate me still? I mean, we'd sacrificed what could've been a wonderful life together for his impossible standards.

And fuck him, it's not like Anne's life ended up going the way he wanted it to, now did it? She didn't end up marrying one of his preferred finance douche bags that he approved of. She ended up marrying a string of even worse assholes that looked more like an act of revenge than it did an actual choice. She was here now, still trying to appease him. And yeah, there was still a lot I knew she wasn't telling me, but that would come in time, right?

As friends, of course. Nothing more.

"It doesn't matter how long you stall," a male voice said from my right.

I jolted a little, not having noticed the guy leaning against one of the massive pillars to my right.

"They'll still be waiting to eat you alive once you get inside," he continued.

Oh shit, that was Cannon Price from the Carolina Reapers.

"Shouldn't you be at a game?" I asked.

"Shouldn't a cop be more perceptive of his surroundings?"

I laughed, nodding. "Touché."

"I have an away game tomorrow," he said.

"I was in my head," I offered.

"Memories?"

I scrunched my brow, heading to stand next to him. "I'm guessing you were around some sister chatting?"

He shrugged. "A little."

"Great."

"Don't worry," he said. "You'll be fine."

"Says the guy who was accepted into the family with open arms."

"Who the fuck told you that story?" Cannon asked, laughing. "It was more like a battle I had to fight to prove myself and hell, I still don't feel worthy of my wife, but she's sure as hell worth the fight."

I blew out a breath. "Not that I'm fighting for my spot or anything, but if a multi-millionaire pro-hockey player struggled for approval, I sure as hell don't stand a chance."

Cannon shook his head and clapped me on the back. "One thing I've learned these last couple months is that it's not the money. It may look like that on the surface, but it's not."

I didn't believe him, but he was trying to be nice so I didn't voice that out loud.

"Did you win last night?" I asked. "I missed the game."

"Yep," he said. "We're on a real streak."

"Nice."

Cannon cocked a brow at me. "You want to keep up the chit-chat? I'm cool with it, if you need to. I get how intimidating VanDoren women can be."

"Anne doesn't intimidate me."

Cannon looked skeptical.

"She's a powerhouse," I said. "No doubt about that. Wild and full of life and..." I shook my head. "But it's never been her that was the issue."

He nodded, understanding flashing over his eyes.

"Has the party started without me?" Another voice sounded behind us, and I glared at the guy I'd seen making Anne laugh at the restaurant last week. Brandon? Brett? "Brad," he said, reaching out a hand.

Cannon shook it first since I made no move to.

"Cannon," he said.

"Persephone's husband," Brad said. "Anne told me all about you. You play for the Reapers. I'm a big fan."

"Thanks."

"And you are?" Brad turned to me, and I know I had absolutely no right to dislike the guy but I fucking did. Anne said they were friends, but one look at him told me he was exactly what her father wanted for her. His suit had to cost more than my car.

"Jim!" Anne's voice came from the now opened front door, Anne and her sister standing in the middle of the entryway. "And Brad?" She smiled at us both as she shared a silent look with Persephone before waving us all inside.

"So good to see you again, Jim," Persephone said, greeting

me with a kind hug that I reciprocated. It had been years since I'd seen her but she'd always been so nice to me.

"Easy," Cannon warned, and I immediately ended the barely two-second hug.

Persephone rolled her eyes and waved him off. "Don't mind him," she said. "He's part caveman."

Cannon grunted without an argument, electing to slide his hand around his wife's waist as they walked toward what I remembered as the formal dining room.

I couldn't believe I'd talked myself into coming to dinner. I must've been out of my fucking mind.

"I brought scotch," Brad said, handing Anne a bottle that looked as old and as expensive as time itself. "I think you father likes that year."

"How thoughtful," Anne said.

"*Shit*," Brad said, cringing slightly as he tucked the bottle under his arm. "Anne, I'm so sorry. I wasn't thinking—"

"It's fine," she said, waving him off, and I tilted my head. What the hell? "No need to pretend like alcohol doesn't exist just because I'm sober."

What. The. Absolute. Hell?

How had I not known that? We'd been working together, had dinner together, and she never once—

"And you brought one of Lyla's pies!" She grinned at the pink box. "Her pumpkin is my absolute favorite." She took the pie from my hands, kissing my cheek in thanks before heading down the hallway after her sister.

I hung back a few seconds, trying to stop myself from chasing her down and asking her all the questions assaulting my brain.

The first being why she didn't trust me enough to tell me what she was going through.

CHAPTER 7

Anne

"**B**rad, my boy," my father greeted Brad with open arms as we all filed into the formal dining room. "So good to see you." They embraced in a quick hug before Father took the scotch Brad offered. "My favorite year," he said, grinning. "Thoughtful of you."

I resisted the urge to roll my eyes. I liked Brad a lot, but in a strictly platonic way. And I'd been shocked to see him on our doorstep moments ago. It was clear my father invited him, likely in the hopes that we'd continue forming a bond. And we were, just not in the way my father wanted.

Father turned toward me after he motioned to Brad's designated seat at the table—right next to mine. What a surprise.

"Who is this?" he asked as he glanced behind me.

Jim took that opportunity to move past me, offering his hand to my father in a gesture that was way kinder than he deserved. Did he not remember how awful my father had been to him or was he just that good a person to let bygones be bygones?

"Jim Harlowe," he said after my father had taken his hand to shake it.

An uncomfortable sort of recollection played out in my father's eyes right before he narrowed his gaze on me. "You invited him."

It wasn't a question, so I didn't feel the need to answer. Instead, I looped my arm through Jim's and guided him around the table, situating him to my left before taking my seat as well. Father helped Mother into her chair before he sat at the head of the table, Cannon and Persephone rounding out our little group.

"This all looks amazing, Mrs. VanDoren," Jim said in his classic polite form.

"Oh, you're a dear," she said, waving him off. "I can't take credit for the feast this year." She sighed. "They wouldn't let me near the kitchen."

Jim nodded. "It's important to rest for your recovery," he said. "Not doing anything strenuous is a crucial part of the process and I'm pretty sure cooking Thanksgiving dinner is the definition of strenuous."

Mom laughed along with the rest of the table. Everyone expect my father, who seemed content to glare at Jim like we were teenagers again.

"What would you know about her recovery," my father asked as he started to carve the turkey.

"The Sweet Water police department ensures we train all the way up to EMT levels," he said. "So I know my way around medical situations. Plus, after I heard the news about Mrs. VanDoren, I looked it up."

He said it so matter-of-factly, as if everyone would do their research regarding a non-relative's situation.

"You're about three weeks out from being able to resume your normal activities, right Mrs. VanDoren?" he asked as if my father hadn't just tried to test him.

"That's right," Mom said, practically beaming. "I can't wait to get in my garden again."

"I'm sure it's missed you," Jim said, taking the platter of green beans Brad passed to him. "You've always had the best flower-gardens in Sweet Water."

We all filled our plates, Sephie and Cannon shooting me worried looks bordering on awkward as their eyes danced from me to Brad to Jim. It certainly would be a hilarious predicament if it was happening to anyone else. Seeing as I was sitting smack dab in the middle of two perfectly handsome, respectable males who were vying for my attention in different ways, I found it a bit less funny.

It was like the universe was showing me two paths. The one my family would prefer me to be on—a luxurious life with Brad—and the one my heart desired, which was any sort of life where I got to see and spend time with Jim every single day.

"I'm so happy you decided to join us today, Jim," Sephie said after the silence at the table had gone one second past comfortable.

"Thanks for having me," he said.

"Must be hard," Father said, stabbing at his turkey. "Not having any family of your own to spend the holiday with."

Mom gasped, and from the look of the movement in her seat, she might've kicked Father under the table.

"I have some extended family," Jim responded calmly. "But they live in Florida."

"And you didn't want to visit them there?" Father asked.

"I love Florida," Brad interjected. "Fantastic golf courses. Which reminds me, Harold, we need to book a tee time soon."

I flashed Brad a grateful look. He was trying to take my father's focus off of Jim, and I kind of loved him for it.

Father nodded at Brad, but kept his focus on Jim while we ate.

"If the Sweet Water police department ever needs any help

with fundraisers or events," Sephie offered, a bite of turkey poised before her lips. "I'd be more than happy to assist. I've been meaning to reach out, but my schedule has been full for some time."

"I have no doubt," Jim said. "Heading up the Carolina Reapers charitable fund sounds like an exciting job. And thank you, I'll be sure to reach out when the next one comes up."

"You're not the sheriff," Father said.

"No, sir, I'm not."

"Do you have any aspirations to be?"

"Not right now," Jim answered, and I shot my father a death glare.

Jim wasn't here as my date but my father was treating him like he was about to ask for my hand in marriage or something. Sweet heavens, could I ever have *one* normal dinner with my family?

I took a deep breath, remembering that most of the uncomfortableness around family gatherings were *my* fault, or had been from quite some time. But I was trying really hard to fix that, to make amends. My father seemed to be trying really hard to make my hate for him grow.

Cannon cocked a brow at my father, then me, a silent offer of help flickering across his features. My heart warmed at the silent offer, at the way he supported me even after the terrible way we started. He'd accepted my apology as easily as Sephie had, and he left it at that. I couldn't ask for a better brother-in-law, and I flashed him a small smile and shook my head. He nodded, then picked up the pitcher of iced tea, refilling Sephie's glass without her having to ask.

The smallest, most annoying stab of jealousy hit me watching the way he took care of her. The way he loved her without conditions or judgment. The way he'd fallen for her naturally without having to be set up by the family. The way they both acted around each other, like two halves of the same whole.

She deserved nothing less, and I was beyond happy for her. I just couldn't help but want that kind of companionship for myself. And I know I shouldn't, because I was in no position to ask anything of the universe. I made my bed and now I was dealing with the consequences. But, someday, maybe I'd be worthy of that kind of love.

"Being a police officer must be time-demanding," my father said after a few moments. "I'm sure you're heading to the station soon, right? It's not like criminals take a day off."

"Father," I hissed, going rigid in my chair.

Jim smiled, shaking his head, while he dabbed at his lips with a napkin despite his mouth and beard being immaculate. A combination of hurt and finality flashed across his eyes as he set down his knife and fork, scooting away from the table.

"You know, you're right," he said, laying his napkin on the table. "Thank you for the meal, Mrs. VanDoren," he continued as he stood up. "It was delicious. I hope you enjoy the pie. I got it from *Lyla's Place*. My friend swears she's the best chef this side of the country."

"Jim," I said, staring up at him. "Please don't go."

"It's all right," he said, glancing at my father. "I'm not where I belong."

The words hit me like a punch to the chest, stunning me for a moment as he walked out of the room.

"*Harold*," Mom chided. "What's gotten into you?"

"That was totally uncalled for," Sephie added.

"Seemed on par to me," Cannon mumbled under his breath before taking another huge bite of turkey.

Finally regaining my senses, I stood up, looking down on my father. "You would think ten years would be enough to erase your unfounded dislike of Jim, but no, you're acting as unreasonable as you did all those years ago. Jim at least had the decency to be polite."

"I—"

"Don't," I cut my father off, flashing an apologetic look at my mother before hurrying out of the room.

I raced through the entryway, catching up to Jim who was waiting for his car at the valet station.

"Jim, wait, please—"

"It's fine, Anne," he said. "Just go back in there and enjoy your Thanksgiving."

"Fuck Thanksgiving," I said, and his eyes flashed wide. "Please, talk to me."

"About what?" he asked, and I tugged on his arm, leading him away from the prying eyes and ears of the valet, and heading deeper into the grounds until we were alone and covered by an outcropping of trees.

"About anything," I said. "I'm so sorry about my father—"

"De ja-fucking-vu," he said, rubbing his palms over his face.

"I didn't think he'd behave the same way after ten years..."

"It's fine," he said. "Seriously. It was a mistake coming here again."

My stomach dropped at his words, and tears welled up in my eyes. "Well, I'm used to that," I finally said, forcing my chin to stay up.

"What?"

"Being a mistake. It's like my unwanted mission statement."

"You are the furthest thing from a mistake," he said, his voice low and rough as he stepped toward me.

"Then what—"

"Me coming here and thinking anything would be different is the mistake. Having any sort of hope that your father would be enlightened was a mistake." He blew out a breath, and I could feel the tension radiating off of him, he stood so close. "Why didn't you tell me about the sobriety?"

"You didn't ask," I said.

"How would I know to ask, Anne?" He gave me a chiding look. "We hadn't spoken for ten years before you came back into my life."

"I know, I'm sorry. I should've told you but..." Why hadn't I brought it up when we first had dinner? When he'd kissed me? The reasoning, as sad as it was, settled in my chest. "I didn't want you to know."

"Why?"

"Because I didn't want you to see my failures any more than you had in the gossip columns that loved to paint my story all over the papers."

"Addiction doesn't make you a failure," he said. "It just means you need help. You know I'd never judge you. I never have—"

"I know," I said. "I *know*. I'm just trying to reorient my life and I'm trying to do better and I didn't know how to open that conversation." I flung my arms out. "Hey, Jim. I'm four weeks sober because the doctors told me if I kept up my habits, I would be dead within the year. Also, I've been an awful person to my sister more times than I can count due to an incident that wasn't even her fault, I've been a coward as much as I've been numb to reality, and I've had a string of failed marriages to men who hated me more than they liked me. Great to see you again."

He gaped at me, his eyes churning as he processed the info dump I'd laid on him.

"Your liver?" he finally asked, and I nodded. He took a step back, raking his fingers through his hair.

"You see why I didn't want to tell you?" I asked, folding my arms over my chest like I could protect myself. "I don't really care what anyone else thinks of me, but you? Your opinion means more to me than anyone else's. And for once, I didn't want to be the mistake or the embarrassment. I just wanted to be...me."

"Why?" he asked. "Why does my opinion matter to you?"

"You know why," I said, my words almost a whisper.

"And Brad," he said, throwing my mind for a loop. "Why was he there?"

"My father invited him, I assume. He's been trying to set us up."

A muscle in his jaw flexed.

"But we're just friends. We decided that the moment we first met."

"You have no interest in him?"

"No," I said. "My father wants that life for me—"

"High school all over again—"

"And he's a great guy," I forged on. "But he's not who I want. He's not *you*," I admitted on a breath.

Jim's eyes snapped to mine, a charged sense of urgency lashing between us. He took one step toward me, then another, like he simply couldn't stand the distance between us. Slowly, he slid his hand over my neck, gliding his fingers through my hair.

"This can never work," he said, gently tugging my hair to tip my head back.

I was practically trembling in his embrace. "You're too good for me," I whispered back.

"Never," he said, his mouth inching down toward mine. "You're the one who I can't touch, who I shouldn't touch."

His lips grazed over mine in a featherlight caress, sending warm shivers all over my body.

"What if I want you to touch me?" I asked, my skin flushing hot.

"You know all you have to do is ask."

Something warm and tight settled in me, my desire a pulsing beacon as he held me suspended there in anticipation.

"Please," I said, begged. "Touch me."

His lips were on mine in an instant, claiming and so damn sweet as he licked into my mouth. I opened for him, my hands flying around his neck to draw him closer. He hooked a strong arm around my waist, hauling me off my feet and backward until I was pressed against the trunk of a tree. He settled me there, never breaking our kiss as he shifted my legs apart with his thigh.

I gasped as he kissed his way to the corner of my mouth, then to the spot just beneath my jaw. Electric tingles soared down my spine, my heart racing as my body lit up every single place he touched.

"Remind me," he said, his voice ragged as his hand traveled down my ribs. "Did I ever make you come?"

Fire licked up my insides at his question, and I met his eyes. We'd only ever done over-the-clothes stuff, and yes, our make-out sessions were hot, especially in the back of his car with him on top of me, but we'd never crossed that line. We didn't have time to.

I shook my head, suddenly feeling nervous and shy in a way I'd never felt before.

He smirked like he knew the answer to the question, but wanted to watch me squirm under it. "Would you like me to?"

My breath stuttered out of my lungs as he dragged his hand lower, teasing it beneath the skirts of my dress.

"Yes," I sighed the answer. "God, yes."

He captured my mouth again, his hand teasing me over the lace I wore. He pulled back again, his green eyes flaring. "You're already so wet," he said. "Fuck, baby, let me take care of you."

My entire body surrendered at his words, at his touch, my mind letting go of every reason we shouldn't be doing this—

least of all that we were completely out in the open. I didn't care, not as long as he kept touching me—

"James!" I gasped as he slipped his fingers beneath the lace, stroking through my heat with just the right amount of pressure. He slanted his mouth over mine, curling those fingers against me until I whimpered between his lips.

He swirled my wetness around my aching clit, teasing me to the point of desperation. I rocked against his hand, chasing my pleasure with an abandon I hadn't felt safe enough to do in so damn long. But this was Jim, and there wasn't a man I trusted more than him.

"This what you want?" he said against my lips, pulling back enough to catch my gaze as he slid in one finger, then two. "Like this?" he asked, curling those fingers inside me, stroking me while keeping the pressure just light enough to keep me riding that sweet edge of release.

"Yes," I moaned, throwing my head back as he continued to pump those fingers inside me. "God, yes."

He grinned, kissing down my neck as he worked me up and up, winding me up so tight I knew I would snap at any moment. "You might want to keep it down, baby," he said, his lips against my neck before returning to my mouth. "Someone could hear."

"I don't care," I said, breathless as I gripped his shoulders, holding on to him like a lifeline. "I don't care who hears us."

And I really didn't. Jim's hands were on me, his mouth, his body flush with mine. The whole world could know and it wouldn't stop me from wanting more, needing more.

"Fuck," he groaned, like my declaration had loosened something inside him. He kissed me again, harder, hungrier, and then he pressed the heal of his palm over that aching bundle of nerves just as he pumped his fingers inside me—

I flew apart.

Shattered into a million glittering pieces.

"James," I moaned into his mouth, and he deepened the kiss like he wanted to devour my cries of pleasure as I trembled around him, each wave stronger than the next, making my body jerk slightly against his.

He worked me through the throes of it, slowing his pace as he dragged out my orgasm until it tapered off into a blissful sort of satisfaction I'd never felt before. Gently, he pulled his fingers from me, settling my dress back around my hips.

I kissed him again, slow and languid and lust-hazy as I slid my hands over his abdomen and down, reaching for the zipper on his pants, fully prepared to return the favor—

"Anne?" Sephie's voice rang from the direction of the house, her tone colored in worry. "Anne, where are you?"

Jim pulled away almost reluctantly.

"They're worried about you," he said.

"I don't care," I argued.

"Yeah you do," he said. "And it's okay. You belong in there, and I belong out there." He motioned toward the drive, where his car was no doubt waiting to take him far away from this place. Far away from me and all the drama I brought to his life.

"Jim, don't say it like that."

"Like what?"

"With such finality."

He parted his lips, but now Cannon was yelling for me, and their voices were getting closer.

"I'm coming!" I yelled back, hoping to appease them long enough for me and Jim to sort this out.

"Again?" he joked, and it did little to lighten the rising panic in me.

He was going to leave and pretend like this never happened. I could sense it as easily as I could sense when he was holding back.

"Try to enjoy the rest of your evening," he said, heading away from me and toward the drive. "I'll see you at work."

And that was that.

He left me standing there, still flushed from what he'd just done to my body, gaping at his back as he walked away.

I shook my head, forcing myself to not let the confusion and worry and doubt steal the one thing his touch had given me—because for the first time in a long time, I didn't feel ashamed or regretful after intimacy.

I felt *seen*.

And that was something to hold on to, even if I'd never experience it again.

CHAPTER 8

Jim

I t'd been a week since Thanksgiving, and I swear I could still taste Anne on my tongue.

I was losing my mind with need.

Every time I closed my eyes, I saw the way her lips curved up as she came on my fingers. Every time I breathed, I caught a whiff of her floral and spice scent.

Every time she spoke to me at work, I heard her sighing my name against my mouth as she flew apart around me.

When she showed up to work the next day, she acted like nothing happened, so I acted like nothing happened, even though we both knew perfectly fucking well what happened.

We'd crossed a line. Hell, we'd obliterated that line. I'd stomped out of that dinner fully aware I'd never be good enough for her...but she'd *chased* me.

She'd come after me.

Something she hadn't done when her father tore us apart all those years ago. Back then, I'd waited for her. I selfishly hoped she'd choose me over her inheritance and her father's demands, but she never came.

Last week she had. Not just for me, but *because* of me, and both ways were driving me to the point of breaking.

I knew we couldn't work.

I knew her father would likely pull the same shit he did a decade ago and she'd have to abide by his rules. I was fully aware that I wasn't worth the millions he had waiting for her, but did any of that matter right now?

No.

Not when I couldn't stop laughing with her, praising her for how great she was doing at work, seeing her the same way I saw her back then only with more depth and appreciation than my teenager self could ever muster.

Even though we were adamantly ignoring the giant, lust-crazed elephant in the room, we'd fallen into such an easy rhythm it was like we'd been working together for years. Which was exactly why I could tell something was wrong with her today.

She'd been tense all day, the set of her shoulders tight, and the tip of her tongue sharp. She kept snapping and then apologizing to me right before her eyes would go distant in a way that told me she wasn't fully here at all. She kept going somewhere else, and I was dying to know where.

My nerves tangled the longer the day went on until it was like I was siphoning off the energy she projected. I think all the new hires noticed too, because they were practically elated to leave once the day was done, so much so they damn near bolted from the door.

I didn't know what was going on, but I didn't want Anne to be alone. Things might be complicated between us, but she was undergoing a crucial part in her life right now and she needed all the support she could get. The last thing I wanted was my attempts to keep distance between us outside of work to drive her into a relapse. God knows her family didn't know her like I did, and had isolated her to the point she had a hard fucking time trusting anyone.

Sure, she and Persephone were mending that old wound between them, but that didn't mean they understood Anne on the level that I did. And maybe I was an arrogant bastard for thinking so, but I felt like I could offer her support in a way they couldn't.

"Anne," I said as she headed for the door.

"Hmm?" she asked, eyes still distant.

"Do you have plans tonight?" My heart screamed at me that this was another bad idea, but I shut that shit down. I could feel it, she needed me. Needed someone who saw her without any of the past wrapped around her.

"Netflix and takeout," she said, shrugging. "Wild times."

I laughed. "How about Netflix and a home-cooked meal?"

She furrowed her brow. "Do you think I learned to cook since I last saw you? Because that's a hard no. I burned Ramen the other day."

I stepped up to her, shaking my head. "I meant me," I said, and she arched a brow at me. "Can I cook for you?"

Her pink lips parted, and it took everything in my power not to reach down and capture them with my own. I was still in uniform for fuck's sake.

"Sure?" she said but it sounded more like a question.

"Great," I said. "Meet me at my place in an hour?" I texted her the address.

"Okay," she said, hope chasing away some of the darkness in her eyes.

A shower and an hour later, I swung open my door to welcome an incredibly delectable Anne, dressed casually in a pair of black yoga pants and an oversized cream sweater. Fuck, I'd seen her in silk dresses and business suits and everything in between but this disarmed version of herself was my new weakness.

"It smells amazing in here," she said, timidly entering my house like it might hold a set of traps that would send her plummeting if she stepped in the wrong spot.

"Make yourself at home," I said, shutting the door behind her before heading back into the kitchen. "I'm just finishing up the sauce."

"Wow," she said, half-laughing as she took in my place. I'd saved up for five years before purchasing the home, and it was one of my most proud accomplishments. My parents had never been able to afford a two-story house before, let alone one that was situated on two acres, and I knew they'd be so proud of me if they could see me.

Did I need five bedrooms? No, not at all.

Did I love every square inch of my house? Absolutely.

Still, it was nothing compared to what Anne had grown up in or what she was accustomed to.

"Your house is so beautiful," she said, finding me in the kitchen at the stove. "I love it."

I grinned from ear to ear, telling my chest not to puff out. "It's got a certain charm," I said, and she nodded as I fixed our plates.

I carried them over to the kitchen table I had tucked against the farthest wall. I had a dining room with a larger table, but living alone, I was used to eating at the smaller one.

"Omigod," she moaned after she took the first bite. "This is amazing."

"It's one of my signature dishes," I said, shrugging as I twirled the creamy pasta around my fork. "It's nothing like Lyla's," I continued. "Or anything like the Michelin star restaurants you're used to eating from, but it's not bad."

"Stop it," she chided me, scooping up another huge bite of the Cajun chicken pasta. "I love it. No one—outside of our chef or my mom—has ever cooked for me before."

"You can't be serious," I said. "Not one of your..." I don't know why I didn't want to say *exes*. Maybe it was because I was worried it would hurt her or maybe it was because I didn't want to acknowledge she'd ever been married before.

"My ex-husbands were assholes," she said without missing a beat. "Not all of them were abusive, but not one of them actually liked me. They were there for the thrill of marrying a VanDoren. A drunken thrill ride with the prospect of a grand prize at the end of it." She shook her head, hanging it a bit lower as she twirled more pasta around her fork. "So no," she continued. "They weren't leaping at the chance to cook for me, but to be fair, it's not like I ever took the time to learn to cook for them either."

I swallowed hard, anger flashing hot through my veins. Worry washed over me at just how far the abuse went with her exes, but I knew she'd tell me if she wanted to talk about it. She deserved better. "Why..." I stopped myself, shaking my head. "Never mind. It's none of my business."

"I'll tell you almost anything you want to know," she said, shocking the hell out of me.

"Almost?" I asked.

She breathed out slowly. "There are some parts of my life I can't even share with my therapist yet," she admitted. "But I'm trying. I really am. I'm working up to it, but..." She clenched her eyes shut, and I reached across the table, laying my hand over hers. "I'm not there yet. Other than that, I'm doing this thing where I'm trying to be as honest as possible, even if it paints me in a bad light."

"I understand," I said, drawing my hand back so she could keep eating. "Is that what was bothering you today?" I asked. "The things you're not ready to talk about?"

"You could tell?" she asked. "Is that a cop trick you learned? To detect when someone is off?"

"No, it's an Anne trick," I answered. "I've always been able to tell when you're off."

"Wow," she said, focusing on her pasta, a soft smile on her lips. "Yes," she admitted. "It was. Sometimes memories just get ahold of me and won't let go. Fighting them off is exhausting sometimes too. But again, I'm trying my best."

"I get that," I said. "And I think you're doing amazing. I know it's not easy."

"Nothing worth it ever is, right?" She took another few bites. "So, you wanted to know why I got married so many times, right? Most of them not even lasting a few months? That's what you were going to ask before."

"Only if you want to tell me," I said. "But yes, I was wondering."

"The time right after you and I broke up was the hardest time I've ever been through," she said. "Not only because I lost you, but because of...other situations. I decided it would be much more fun to escape into a fantasy land than live in reality. I tried to drown out memories I couldn't erase, and spent my time traveling in an attempt to outrun my past. I thought if I could get enough distance between this place and me, I would magically get better. I thought if I partied hard enough, I would actually start to believe that I was living my best life. I thought that if I was married, I wouldn't have to think about how alone I felt."

I set down my fork, no longer hungry, my appetite replaced by a deep sadness for the girl I used to love. She'd been full of life with aspirations to travel and research the countries' histories before one day settling down here in Sweet Water. What awful thing had happened between the time we broke up to the year she left to turn her world on its axis so much?

My gut whispered an answer, but I didn't want it to be true, and I certainly wouldn't ask her until she was ready to talk about it.

"So, yeah," she said. "That's why I got married so many

times. And spoiler alert, none of those things actually worked."

"And you came back here anyway," I said. "Even though you were determined to stay away."

She nodded, blowing out a breath. "My sister's wedding," she said. "And my mother's failing kidney brought me back. The fact that Sephie had gotten married during a weekend in Vegas made me think maybe she wasn't as perfect as she always seemed. That maybe, just maybe, we were alike in all the ways I used to feel like we were. But, in true Persephone form, her mistake turned into a goldmine. And in true Andromeda form, I tried to ruin it for her. Tried to turn her hasty marriage into something closer to my own mistakes." She wrung out her hands.

"I was awful," she continued. "Wanting her to be as broken as me. Wanting to expose her marriage like one of my mistakes. And then after, when I realized how much Cannon loved her, how madly in love they both were...I snapped. Hitting rock bottom is an actual thing and it happens more than just once. It feels like you've jumped off a ledge. Every-thing hurts when you realize what you've done, what your addiction helped you do." She looked down at her hands.

"When I tried to get tested to see if my kidney was a match for my mother's is when the doctors told me about my liver, told me I might not live to see another year if I didn't make a giant life-change, but asking my sister for help was more of a breakthrough than even finding that out. Mending those wrongs between us, wrongs she doesn't even understand, means more to me than even healing my scarred liver." She finally looked up at me. "And my mother," she said. "Knowing she's okay and is going to live, I feel like I have a second chance to make her proud. To right the wrongs I've done to her in the past. But my father..."

I swallowed around the knot in my throat, hating that I

didn't have the right words to respond. I thought she'd been living a wild, care-free life traveling across the globe like she always wanted to, but she'd been suffering in ways I couldn't even imagine.

"I don't know if I'll ever be able to forgive him. But I'm trying to at least earn back his respect." She shrugged, taking a sip of her ice water. "Sometimes that seems a harder task than staying sober."

I flinched. "It shouldn't be that way with family."

"VanDorens," she said in a mocking tone. "Anyway," she continued, trying to brush off the seriousness of the conversation if her smile was any indication. "Not all his stipulations of earning my way back into the family's good graces are bad."

"Oh yeah?" I asked. "Like what?"

"Working with you for one," she said. "Working for Lyla for two. I never thought I would enjoy waiting tables as much as I do. Maybe it's because I've never done it before or maybe it's because I never knew how satisfying a hard day's work could feel. Either way, that is one thing I don't regret about this whole process. And my studio apartment is cozy, even if I can barely turn around in it."

I laughed, trying to protest when she stood up to clear our finished plates. I watched her as she rinsed and put them in the dishwasher, the actions so domestic it made it hard to breathe. It was like I'd fallen into one of my painful fantasies where we lived happily ever after and cleaning up after dinner was a normal, everyday occurrence for us.

"Is there anything you do regret?" I asked her after I stored the leftovers in the fridge.

She leaned against my kitchen island, and I made sure I kept my distance against the counter across from her. "About the stipulations from my father?" she asked, and I nodded. "Not really. Therapy is hard sometimes, even though I know it's one of the main elements keeping me out of a rehabilitation facility. And as much as I love Dr. Casson, it's hard to crack open about how you've failed your family more times than you can even remember."

"You're not a failure," I said, and she laughed.

"My long line of mistakes begs to differ."

I pushed off the counter, needing to be just a little closer to her when I said what I wanted to say. "Your mistakes don't define you," I said, looking down at her.

We were so close I could feel the heat coming off her body. God, I wanted to drag her into my arms and feel her against me.

"You're brilliant," I continued, and gently tipped her chin when she tried to look away from me. "You have the best sense of humor. You don't take shit from anyone regardless if they're ten times your size or not. You have an attitude big enough to fill all of Sweet Water but your compassion for those you *do* let in is just as fierce. You're an incredible woman, Anne. And no amount of things in your past could change that."

Her lips parted, emotion shifting her features from awed to doubtful to confused. "How do you see me like that?"

"I've always seen you."

A shaken breath rushed past her lips, and I swear there was a buzz of electricity crackling between us. I couldn't deny the tension coiling inside me, couldn't ignore the overwhelming sensation I had to hold her, kiss her, be with her. Chemistry like this came along once in a lifetime, I knew that since the day we broke up. And even though I knew there wasn't a world where we worked out, I wanted to *try*.

"James," she breathed my name, and I had to brace my hands on either side of her, gripping the kitchen island like it would help me maintain control. "Tell me what you're thinking, please."

I licked my lips, my eyes scanning every inch her face from

her pink lips to her fluttering blue eyes. "I'm thinking working with you every single day is absolute torture."

Shock flared in her eyes, so I hurried to continue.

"Standing there every day, pretending like I can't stop thinking about you is driving me crazy. You're in my head all the time, in all the ways I want to touch you, kiss you, make you come so many times I'll be the comparison for everyone who comes after me. Because I know this can't work, but it doesn't stop me from needing you on a level that terrifies me."

Her hands flew to my chest, fisting the material of my shirt to draw me closer. "I'm still a mess," she admitted, reaching up on her tiptoes to bring her mouth closer to mine.

I gripped her hips and hefted her onto the island, separating her thighs to step between them.

"I'm still healing," she continued, sliding her hands over my shoulders, her eyes fluttering from my eyes to my lips and back again.

"I know," I said, fully understanding she was working on herself in ways that would take up all the energy she had. I knew she didn't need me to help her heal, but I damn sure would be there for her while she did it. "And I want to be here for you. Support you in whatever way you need." She bit her bottom lip, hesitance and need churning in her eyes. "I know I'm not what your family wants and that you're trying to mend things with them. I get that. It doesn't change how I feel about you. And this doesn't have to be the end-all. We can just *be*."

"So just this once?" she asked, and my heart fucking rebelled at the idea. Once would never be enough with her. But if that's all she wanted, then that's what I'd give her.

"One night?" I asked, wanting absolute clarity between us.

"Whatever you want," she said, echoing my thoughts.

"I just want you," I admitted, inching my way toward her mouth.

"You have me."

I slanted my mouth over hers, sweeping my tongue between her lips until she let me in. Her grip on me tightened, and she wrapped her legs around my waist, locking me in place against her. My dick strained at the move, hard and desperate to sink into her. I tangled my fingers in the silken strands of her hair, kissing her deeper—

"Wait," she said, pulling back just enough to catch my eyes.

I froze, telling my dick to stand the fuck down. I would never have her doing anything she wasn't comfortable with. If she wanted to just make-out like we were teenagers again, then that's what we'd do. If she wanted to sit there and talk until the sun came up, I was fine with that too.

"I'm..." She worried her lip between her teeth again.

"What is it, baby?"

"I'm nervous," she admitted, and my eyes flared wide. My wild, ferocious girl was nervous?

"Why?"

"I haven't had sex in over a year," she said. "And I wasn't exactly in a state to remember it. What if I'm not...what if you don't like..."

She struggled with her words, and I shook my head. She could've slipped on that confident, downright dominant mask she normally wore and demanded I get on my knees for her. She could've pretended like this was nothing more than a one-night stand to her, but she was choosing to be honest with me, and that touched me in a way that was dangerous to my heart.

"What if I'm not good." She clenched her eyes shut. "I haven't had sex sober. *Ever.*"

"Look at me," I said, and she slowly opened her eyes. "You are exquisite. The definition of desire. I look at you and I'm hard. I look at you and I want nothing more than to sink deep inside you and feel you come around my cock. You're everything I've ever wanted. Never doubt that."

Her eyes fluttered, and she kissed me, soft and tender, almost like a thank you.

"Still nervous?" I asked, and she nodded almost sheepishly.

I smirked, placing my hands on her thighs. "Let me take care of you."

She nodded, the consent all I needed to hook my hands into the band of her yoga pants. I tugged, and she lifted her luscious ass, allowing me to roll the pants down her long legs and toss them over my shoulder. The scrap of lace she wore came off next, then her shirt and bra, and my shirt and pants, all landing in a chaotic pile behind me between frantic kisses.

"Fuck," I said, taking my time scanning her bare body. She really was exquisite, all sweeping curves and stunning breasts that begged to fill my hands, and a thin beautiful strip of blonde curls acting as a beacon guiding me to where I needed to taste her most. "You're beautiful."

Her hands traced the lines of my abdomen, her eyes wide and hungry. I'd never been so happy about all the time I spent in the gym. If it made her look at me like that, I would put an in-home gym in the basement and work out every fucking day.

She traveled lower, reaching between us to grip me over my boxer-briefs. I hissed, jerking my hips as I rocked into her hand. Her grip felt so fucking good, but this wasn't about me right now. This was about her.

I nipped at her lip, breaking our kiss to work my way down her neck, over her collarbone, until I reached her breasts. I massaged one with one hand, gripping the other and teasing her nipple with my tongue until it was pert. I did the same with the other one, taking my time between the two, worshiping every inch of her since we'd only agreed on one night. I'd take my time with her, and I wouldn't waste a single second of it.

She arched her back to give me better access, and slowly, I kissed my way down her curves, shifting down until I could kiss her inner thighs.

Her breathing hitched as I kissed her everywhere but where she was glistening for me. Her thighs clenched in anticipation, and just when I thought she might scream at me, I licked her from entrance to clit.

"*James*," she whimpered, and my dick got that much harder at the sound of my name on her tongue. I licked her again, her flavor bursting on my tongue. She was so fucking sweet. I'd never get enough.

I gripped her thighs, spreading her farther, and she laid back on the island in the sexiest move of submission and trust I'd ever seen. I teased the swollen nub of her clit, spearing the bundle of nerves with just enough pressure to make her arch into my mouth before drawing away.

She reached down, her fingers gripping my hair as I feasted on her, plunging my tongue inside her and curling it before pulling out to circle her clit. Her thighs were trembling, so I situated them over my shoulders, never stopping for a second.

"Omigod," she breathed as I worked her up and up, relishing the taste of her with every swipe. "Your *mouth*."

I smirked against her heat, pulling back just enough to glance up at her. She looked down her body at me, our eyes locking in a primal gaze that had my dick jumping.

"Still nervous?" I asked again.

She pressed her lips together, nodding.

"Let's take care of that then, shall we?"

I didn't give her time to answer.

I unleashed myself on her, lapping and plunging in every way that made her moan. Her grip tightened in my hair, her hips arching of the table as she chased the pressure she so desperately needed. I held her on the edge for only a few seconds more, no longer able to stop myself.

I shifted, replacing my tongue with two fingers, stroking her while I sucked her clit into my mouth.

"James!" A strained whimper escaped her lips right after my name, her thighs tightening as she bucked against my hand and mouth. Warmth coated my fingers as she pulsed around them, her orgasm making her entire body tremble.

It was the sexiest thing I'd ever seen.

I worked her down with gentle strokes, shifting her legs off of me as I stood up fully, slipping an arm beneath her lower back to haul her up so we were face to face.

"Still nervous?" I asked.

Her chest heaved as she caught her breath, her entire body looking relaxed and pliant for me. Her eyes were lust-laced as she smiled and shook her head. "Not even a little bit."

"Good," I said, kissing her quickly as I moved her arms to wrap around my neck. "Then lock your ankles."

CHAPTER 9

Anne

I'd never wrapped my legs around a man so fast in all my life. The demand in Jim's tone was enough to have me liquid again, and he'd just made me come.

With his *mouth*.

Usually, I was the one to take the reins. Even in a drunken stupor, I had to control everything. It was my way of keeping myself safe.

But not here.

Not with him.

I trusted him down to the very core of my being, and it was freeing to hand myself over to him and know without a doubt he'd take care of me.

"Good girl," he said, and a drop of pure, melted honey slid down my spine at the praise. He hauled me off the kitchen island without effort, spinning us as he walked through his home, and up the stairs to what I quickly realized was his bedroom.

I told him I wasn't nervous, and when he asked moments ago, that was the truth. But now, as he laid me on his bed with such tenderness I wanted to cry, the butterflies from earlier were back. I wasn't lying when I said I couldn't remember the last time I had sex—not fully, anyway. Everything was coated in a film of alcohol, and without it, I could feel everything in high definition.

Every touch.

Every kiss.

Every graze of his fingers over my sensitive skin.

My body reacted for him in a way it never had for anyone else, and *damn* did I love the way it felt.

I scooted backward on the bed as he climbed atop it, stalking toward me like a predator would its prey. But not one inch of me felt unsafe, and that was refreshing in a way I couldn't articulate. I wanted him to know how much this meant to me, how much he meant to me, but I couldn't possibly find the right words.

So, I decided to show him.

He laughed as I pounced, using my legs to urge him to flip over on his back. It was my turn to take my time eying his body, which was tons of corded muscle under smooth skin. Sweet heavens, he looked like all he did in his spare time was work out.

I trailed my fingers over a couple of tattoos scrawled over his chest, the black whorls of ink a beautiful kind of abstract artwork. I replaced the exploration with my mouth, kissing my way down his chest, the hard ridges of his abdomen, until I hooked my fingers in his black boxer-briefs and slid them down his legs.

Holy. Shit.

My entire body flushed with anticipation at the sight of his cock springing free of the material. He was big, so big I knew it would hurt so damn good before I adjusted to him.

"*James*," I said, my lips parting. We had only ever done PG-13 stuff when we were teenagers, so I had no idea what I was in store for here. This...wow.

I wrapped my fingers around his cock, delighting in the warm silkiness as I stroked him up and down. He hissed, lifting his hips to rock into my hand, and I lowered my head, smiling up at him before I flicked my tongue over his head.

"Fuck," he groaned, arching his head back against the pillows.

I trailed my tongue up and down his shaft before sucking the tip of his cock into my mouth.

"Anne," he growled as I sucked and pumped him at the same time.

He was far too big to take all the way in, but I did my best as I bobbed up and down on him. A little thrill burst down my spine at every sound he made, every clench of his muscles as I did my best to show him how much he meant to me, to show him I wanted him just as much as he wanted me.

"Fuck, baby," he said, his fingers flying to my hair as I upped my pace, humming slightly around him in response. "I need you up here," he said, if not demanded as he gently tugged at my hair.

I drew back, licking my lips as I crawled up his delicious body to settle over him. I stayed up on my knees, straddling him just enough that I could grip him between us. "You need me here?" I asked, my voice emboldened by the position I was in. I dragged his slick head through my heat, rewarded by his groan.

"Fuck," he said, gripping my hips. "Yes. Do that again."

I did. Over and over, I slid him between my legs without actually taking him in, working us up so hard and fast sweat glistened on our bodies.

"Goddamn, Anne," he said. "You're amazing." In one quick movement, he hauled me around, switching our positions in a blink.

My spine kissed the mattress, and he leaned over to his nightstand, rolling a condom on faster than I could catch my breath. He settled between my thighs, holding himself up with one arm by my head, the other massaging my hip.

"Are you sure?" he asked, and I melted a little more.

"Absolutely," I said, and rolled my hips against him for good measure.

His eyes shuttered before he slanted his mouth over mine, kissing me, the taste of me still coating his tongue.

Slowly, he guided himself to my heat, inching in just a bit.

I moaned, gripping his back, my heart racing. I was so sensitive, so stretched out with need I knew it was only going to be seconds before I came again. *He* did that to me. Walked me right up to the edge only to dance with me there like we had all the time in the world. It made me ultra-sensitive to every single move he made, every worshiping touch or claiming kiss.

"How's this?" he asked, sinking in another inch, going slow to give my body time to adjust to the size of him.

"God, yes," I answered, urging him in farther by hooking a leg around his lower back.

"Fuck, baby," he said. "I'm trying to go slow."

I reached up and kissed him, sucking his bottom lip into my mouth before releasing it. "I don't need you to go slow. I need you to fuck me."

He trembled above me. "So demanding." He smirked, sliding an arm beneath my lower back, hauling my hips up higher so he could slide in at a deeper angle until he bottomed out inside me.

"James," I moaned, arching against him. God, he felt good. All hard heat inside me, filling me and stretching me in the best possible way. "Yes." I rolled my hips, taking liberties from the angle he held me in, rocking against him while he held absolutely still.

"God, you feel good," I said, clinging to him as I chased

my pleasure, feeling it build and swirl inside me until I could almost taste it.

He pulled all the way out only to glide right in again. "You feel amazing," he said, doing it over again. "All slick and hot for me."

My breath hitched, every pump from him at that angle driving me closer and closer to release. He drew back enough to look down between us, his eyes flaring at where we connected only to return focus to me.

"Look at you," he said, pumping into me, watching every expression that fluttered over my face. "Look at how well you take my cock."

Sweet heavens, this man was going to be the end of me. How could he possibly be the perfect combination of proper southern politeness during the day and proper sinful delight at night?

He drew all the way out, leaving just the tip in for a few moments until I looked down between us. Lava streaked through my veins at the sight, at the way he was playing my body like an instrument he'd mastered. He plunged in again, sending heat spiraling all throughout my body, plucking every nerve ending awake with the sweetest song.

Over and over, he sank into me before pulling out, stringing me up with crackling need that threatened to consume me.

I was his to play.

I was his to own.

I was his in a way I'd never been anyone else's.

"You're there," he said, his voice as ragged as my breathing. "I can feel you clenching me so damn good."

I pulsed around him, my pleasure on the cusp of exploding. "James, I'm...I'm..."

I couldn't make out the words. I couldn't think straight. Not when he bottomed out and ground against my oversensitive clit. Not when he hauled me as close to him as humanly possible and pistoned his hips—

"God," I moaned as pleasure ripped from my body, splintering me in the most beautiful way. Warmth slicked my thighs as he pumped me from one orgasm right into another, drawing out the pleasure until I cried out his name.

"Fuck," he groaned, chasing my orgasm with his own until he gently rolled us to our sides as we caught our breath.

Apprehension washed over me, threatening to steal every ounce of joy inside me at the moment. My body remembered this moment, remembered that now was the time he'd hop out of bed and hunt down a drink or a hit or a shower.

I clenched my eyes shut, forcing the thoughts from my head. Those memories weren't of Jim. Weren't of anyone who ever actually cared about me.

"Hey," he said, gently stroking back my hair. "Did I hurt you?"

I opened my eyes, my heart melting at the concern in his.

"Not even close," I said, and relief shaped his features.

He scooted close to me, kissing me quickly before he *did* hop out of bed.

My heart sank, a balloon bursting in my chest as he hurried into what I assumed was a connected bathroom. It wasn't like I'd gotten a good look at his room when we came up here. Now would be a good time to find my clothes, but they were downstairs. Still, it's not like I wanted to lay here naked in his bed while he showered me off of himself—

"On your back," Jim demanded, and my eyes flared wide as I did what I was told. And watched as he tenderly, almost lovingly cleaned me up before returning to the bathroom, only to bring back a glass of water and hand it to me. "Drink up," he said.

I raised my brows but sat up enough to drink half the glass

down. His approving smile was enough to make warm shivers dance beneath my skin.

"Do you need something to eat?" he asked, and I tilted my head.

"No, why?" I asked as he took the water from me and sat it on his nightstand.

"Because I'm nowhere near close to finished with you yet."

My lips parted, but I couldn't form a response as he climbed back onto the bed. His kiss was slower this time, almost lazy, as if we indeed had all the time in the world to play.

He gently pushed me back onto the bed, bringing our bodies flush as he seemed content to kiss the breath straight from my lungs.

And as I fell deeper and deeper under his spell, I knew without a doubt that I was wholly and truly fucked.

Because I already knew I was falling in love with this new version of myself, but now...

Now I was certain I was falling for him again.

And I didn't have a clue what to do about it.

CHAPTER 10

Jim

"Are you feeling okay?" I asked, noting the way Anne wore exhaustion like one of her favorite pieces of jewelry.

"Hmm?" she asked, blinking out of a daze she'd held for the last five minutes.

"You've been standing in this hallway for a while now," I said, motioning to the empty coffee cup in her hand, the half-full pot untouched on the small table in front of her.

"Have I?" Something like concern flashed over her features, but she schooled the emotions away with a soft smile. "I didn't realize."

I stepped closer to her. "I know it's been a long week," I said. "But if I'm working you too hard, let me know."

It had been a long week, but a fun one. Even though we hadn't crossed any more lines, we'd fallen right back into our working rhythm, eating lunches together and laughing and getting to know each other again. So much of her was the same, but she had a world of experiences that I practically lapped up when she told me about them.

Sure, some of her past was clouded with a darkness I wasn't yet privy to, but some of it sounded like one big adventure. Her family might not see her the way I do, but damn, she was one hell of a woman. She'd picked up three languages during her travels, not to mention stories upon stories about different cultures. She'd always been fascinated with the history of the world, and in between her string of mistake—as she liked to call them—she'd done her best to chase the dream she had when she was younger.

I admired her all the more for it, and while I loved the friendship we had found our way back to, I couldn't stop thinking about our one-night agreement from last week.

"You're not working me too hard," she finally said, blowing out a breath.

"Are you taking too many shifts at Lyla's?" I asked, more than ready to convince her to take a break. A light dusting of purple swept under her eyes that had my gut churning. She looked drained in a way I'd never seen before. Anne was the epitome of *go-go-go*, barely able to sit still, and today she looked like she was running on empty.

"No," she said, visibly swallowing. An alarm buzzed on her watch, and something clicked behind her eyes. "Damn it." She spun on her heels, heading back to the now empty training room, the new hires having just left after the long day.

I followed her, brow furrowed. "Anne," I said, practically *begged*. "What's going on?"

"It's nothing," she said, almost like she was trying to convince herself. She dug through her purse, but slumped against the desk like she'd been hit with a wave of dizziness.

"Whoa," I said, instantly at her side. I slid an arm around her waist, shifting her into me so I could support her weight.

"Sorry," she said, closing her eyes as she allowed me to hold her. "I forgot to take my medication," she explained, sucking in a deep breath and spinning in my arms to dig in her bag again. "And I haven't eaten much today. I just forgot on both counts."

"And that affects you?" I asked. I'd done a little research on her condition after she'd told me about it on Thanksgiving, but liver damage wasn't my expertise.

"Sometimes," she said, shrugging as she popped a couple of pills in her mouth, grabbing her water bottle from the table and taking a drink. "The doctor said it's to be expected." She shifted against me, trying to wave me off, but I gently held her in place.

"Anne," I said, scanning the tired lines of her face. "Can I help you? Send me your med schedule and I'll set reminders in my phone too. And I'll make sure I have better snacks here for you." We had a small coffee station with an array of packaged snacks, but none of them were likely what she needed, I was now realizing. I'd bring in fruits, veggies, and some healthy carbs tomorrow. I'd read that lowering the sodium intake was helpful with liver damage too.

She smiled, some light coming back to her eyes, like the simple act of taking the medication had cleared some fog laying over them. Moving her hands over my chest, her fingers lingered there, and I couldn't stop my dick from jumping at the simple touch.

One week.

It had been a week since I'd tasted her, touched her, but it felt like a lifetime. We'd agreed on one night, but it wasn't enough. It would never be enough.

"You're a cinnamon roll," she said, grinning up at me. "You know that?"

"Um...thank you?" I posed it like a question, not exactly sure if that was a good thing or not.

A light laugh escaped her lips. "It's a compliment," she explained. "You're always so sweet, so thoughtful with me."

"It's instinct when it comes to you," I said, and she drew a little closer.

Dangerous.

This was incredibly dangerous.

We'd managed to stay professional and safe with each other all week, but here, holding her like this, it made me want to break every boundary we'd silently put in place. We couldn't keep doing this to each other—crashing together when we were inevitably meant to be torn apart.

Right?

Sure, this week had felt like a new normal edged with a hope for more, but that was me living in a fantasy world. Her family would never accept me, and she deserved a life where she didn't have to constantly choose between her family and her partner. A life that didn't involve fighting her father at every single turn when it came to me.

And she was still healing, working through so many different things it would be selfish of me to even ask her to consider fighting for me.

"Do you want to have dinner tonight?" she asked, just like she'd done two other times this week on the nights she wasn't working at Lyla's.

And every time I'd said no, trying to protect us both. Because I knew if I got my hands on her again, there would be no pulling us apart. No amount of hate from her father would be able to keep me away from her.

"I don't think it's a good idea," I said, every word searing my chest as it came out. She was the best idea in the world, but me barging into her life and demanding she make space for me that she didn't have? That wasn't fair.

Her shoulders dropped, and she took a step out of where I'd still been holding her.

"Okay," she said, gathering her bag. Her phone chimed in her purse, and she dug it out, swiping open a text. She turned the phone toward me.

Brad: Hungry? I'm free in twenty if you want to grab dinner.

Jealousy shot through my veins, clenching my muscles. They were friends, she'd told me that, but Brad had a coveted, respected spot in her family's good graces, and I hated him for it on principle.

"Any reason I should tell him no?" she asked, clearly giving me another chance to change my mind. To tell her that the last thing I wanted was her spending time with him instead of me. To tell her that every time we went our separate ways this week it was all I could do to keep myself from texting her and begging her to come over.

I cleared my throat, and shook my head. "Have fun," I said.

God, I was an asshole.

But she deserved better. So much better.

She sighed, dropped her phone in her purse, and headed toward the door. "You too, *James*," she called over her shoulder, the attitude I loved so much about her curling around the formal version of my name, the one she mainly used while I was making her moan. Fuck me.

I stood in the training room far longer than necessary and long after she left, terrified if I took one step in her direction, I'd grab onto her and never let go.

* * *

"It's not our night," Ridge said by way of answer when I knocked on his door.

"Are you saying you're busy?" There was every chance he could be. He had a steady number of women dying for his attention on a weekly basis—something about his tattoos and no-bullshit attitude, I think. Sometimes he indulged one or two of them, sometimes he didn't.

Ridge opened the door to his tattoo parlor, motioning me inside. We headed up the stairs to his loft apartment, and he immediately reached for a beer, offering it to me.

I shook my head, and he cracked it open for himself.

"Solidarity?" he asked.

"Yeah," I answered, used to his one-worded conversations. I didn't have to be sober just because Anne was, but ever since she told me about her condition and the addiction that caused it, I didn't want a drink.

"Interesting," he said, taking a swig as he headed to his couch in the connected living room.

I took a seat across from him in the lone chair he had. "What's interesting?"

"That you're supporting her by not drinking, and yet you're here with me and not out with her."

"It's not a good idea," I said for probably the hundredth time. Ridge wasn't Anne's biggest fan, but after the last couple weeks and everything I'd told him about falling further in friendship with her, he'd lightened up.

"Sure," he said. "You keep telling yourself that." He rolled his eyes, taking another drink.

"Want to order a pizza?"

Ridge shrugged. "I could eat."

I pulled out my phone, ordering our usual.

"Wow," he said after I put my phone away.

"What?"

"You really are content to hide out here with me instead of chasing down the girl of your dreams?"

My mouth hung open, confusion sliding over my face. "Suddenly you're team Anne?"

He grunted. "I'm team Jim," he said. "As ridiculous as that sounds. And I've never seen you as happy as I have in the past few weeks. Do I think it could all end badly?" he nodded. "Sure, but that doesn't mean you shouldn't try."

"I've told you a hundred times why it can't work."

"Yeah, and those reasons may have made sense when you were teenagers, but you're a grown ass man, even if you're acting like a child."

"Ouch," I said. "Maybe I'll take my pizza to go."

Ridge shrugged again, and I contemplated chucking something at his head. It'd be pointless, though. He'd just catch it and throw it back.

"I'm just saying," he said. "If I had a shot at whatever the hell has been making you all moony-eyed lately, I wouldn't be sleeping on it."

I burst out laughing. "That's hilarious," I said. "Remind me which relationship of yours lasted past breakfast?"

"I've never loved anyone like you love her," he said, eying me. "Probably never will. But if I found a person who made me as half as excited to go to work as you've been? Just to see her?" he shook his head, taking another sip of his beer. "You wouldn't be able to stop me from shooting my shot."

"Even if you knew it was doomed from the start?" I leaned my elbows on my knees. "Even if you knew that you'd only end up right back where you started, heartbroken and alone?"

Ridge looked over at me, tilting his head. "I guess you have to ask yourself if the time with her would be worth the pain."

"She's worth everything," I immediately said, and he grinned like the Cheshire Cat, a rarity from my default-grumpy-setting friend.

"I rest my case," he said.

"You're a dick," I said, laughing.

"Yeah, but I'm a dick who's usually right."

I rolled my eyes but couldn't argue, and as much as I wanted to sprint out of his place and track Anne down, I stayed seated. He may be right, but that didn't mean she felt the same way. She might've been totally content with our one-night deal we made last week. That might've been enough for her.

And until I felt otherwise, I couldn't push her.

CHAPTER 11

Anne

"So your father is still pushing really hard for a romantic relationship with Brad?" Dr. Casson asked me.

"Yes," I answered, sighing as I settled more comfortably into my chair. I'd lost count of what session we were on, but each one was getting better and better.

I no longer felt that intense need to defend myself or deflect on any particular question. Dr. Casson had more than earned my trust, never once showing me any sort of judgment but instead offering me an insight to myself I'd never had before.

"And how are the feelings you're having for Jim affecting the already strained situation with your father?"

"We haven't really spoken much since the disaster at Thanksgiving," I said, anger flaring at the memory. "I honestly don't understand how my father can be so disdainful toward Jim. When we were teenagers? Sure, okay, I get it. He was a father trying to protect my future and assumed our relationship was nothing more than a young, fleeting love." He still didn't have to be such an asshole about it. "But now?" I shook my head. "I know I've made mistakes in my life. I'm owning that, as much as it hurts. But I'm an adult, and Jim is absolutely the nicest, most sincere and compassionate person I've ever met."

"And you wish those qualities would matter to your father over titles and positions," she said.

"Yes." I nodded, waving a hand toward her. "You get it. You get *me*." It was refreshing and gave me a sense of solidarity where so many other aspects of my life left me crumbling.

Dr. Casson smiled, her lips painted a pretty shade of hot pink today, giving some fun life to her white silk blouse and black pencil skirt outfit.

"I appreciate that," she said, taking a sip from the water on her desk.

"I'm doing everything my father is asking of me," I continued. "Not that what he's asking is outrageous. I've messed up. A lot. I get it. But the least he could do is give me some credit. Jim isn't like any of my exes, and it's not like I'm trying to marry the guy. We're just..."

What were we? It's not like we'd talked about it before we had our one-night agreement, and we hadn't done anything remotely close to that again. I kept trying, kept asking for more time with him, but he kept shutting me down—in that nice, sweet way of his. Did I know he'd be a thousand times better off without me attached to him? Yes, I did. Did I selfishly want to be worthy of a love like his? Also, yes.

"You have been tackling your father's demands like a form of atonement," she said, brow pinching slightly. "But I hope you realize that the success you're having in your life right now —the sobriety, the accomplishments, the mending of relationships with most of your family—that has nothing to do with your father's demands."

I tilted my head, totally confused. "If he hadn't forced me to secure a job, an apartment, all of it..." I couldn't finish the end of that sentence. I didn't know where I'd be, but the therapy that was helping me in all facets of my life? That was all Sephie, not my father. That made this process nothing but a warm, welcomed experience for me, while the other demands were shrouded in a cold indifference because of the person forcing them on me.

"You still would've come to me," she said when I didn't continue. "Because of your sister, right? She recommended me." I nodded, and she gave me a soft smile. "And you've been doing the hard work in here," she continued. "As much as working at Lyla's and doing volunteer work at the station is changing your outlook on life, in here is where you've been struggling the most." She tapped the end of her pen against the center of her chest. "And here." She moved the pen to her temple.

"I know you're right," I said. Waiting tables wasn't easy. Working for Jim wasn't easy. Paying my own way for the first time in my life wasn't easy. I loved the challenge in all of it, but working on myself? That was the most difficult thing I'd ever done in my life.

"As much as you're owning what you conceive as your failures in life," she said, "you need to own that you're doing so well now because of you. Not because of your father or his demands. Not because of the new friendship with Brad or the budding prospects of a relationship with Jim. Not even because of the encouragement and support from your sister. This is all *you*."

Tears of gratitude filled my eyes, and I tried to laugh them off and brush them away. "I don't think anyone has ever spoken to me like that before," I said. "No one outside of Jim."

Something like sadness weighed in her eyes before she smoothed it away, replacing it with a professional mask of non-bias. "That is unfortunate," she said. "But you can't control other people's reactions to you or your choices. You've learned that here, and have utilized the tools I've given you to help you with your progress. It's time for you to start seeing yourself as the worthy individual you are instead of the troubled, dark mark on the VanDoren name that your family has made you feel like for all these years."

I sucked in a deep breath, shaking my head. "It's not all their fault," I admitted. "I know that now. After what happened...I didn't realize what I was doing, but after seeing you so many times and digging into my past, I can see what I was doing. Trying to erase and outrun something that I'd never be able to face and blaming everyone else around me and taking it out on them when they had no responsibility in the matter at all."

Guilt sank heavy against my chest, the brutal sting all too real without the slow, numbing burn of an alcohol haze. The craving tickled the back of my throat, whispering promises of an escape into my ear. It never went away, that initial reaction to reach for something that would quiet my mind, but I'd gotten a hell of a lot better at acknowledging it and then putting it in its place.

My addiction would never go away, but the way I reacted to it could change. I'd proven that. Some days felt impossible while others were as easy as breathing. I just had to take it one day at a time.

"Are you referring to your sister?" she asked.

"Mainly," I answered. "I took it out on her the most." I cringed at the flood of memories that raced through my mind, a succession of sugary insults or downright ruthless behavior against my sister who was completely innocent in the matter.

I took a deep breath. I was making amends, and she'd already graciously forgiven me without even knowing my motivation behind all the awful things I'd done.

"My father..." I continued. "Some of the things I did to

spite him, yes. And I'm not all that sorry for it." I shrugged. "He constantly pitted me against and compared me to Persephone, even when it was clear we were two entirely different people. I don't know if that is why he doesn't like me as much or if it's because I couldn't shape myself into her carbon copy." I shook my head. "Either way, it only agitated the situation about ten times more after…"

I let the statement hang there, my entire body clenching at the memory.

"Are you ready to open up to me about the incident?" Dr. Casson asked gently. "You've referred to it so many times in our past conversations like it was a catalyst for the spiral you admit to falling into right after."

Ice coated my skin, my heartbeat kicking up a few notches at her direct question. Would explaining what happened help me move on from it? Would it somehow unhook its claws from me?

I honestly didn't know, but I'd never told anyone before, and Dr. Casson had more than proved she was trustworthy. I just…God, I was terrified she'd hear my story and then accuse me of being a child for reacting the way I did toward my family, toward my sister.

"If you're not ready—"

"I am," I blurted out, surprising even myself. "I've never told anyone before," I admitted. "And I'm not going to lie, I'm a little afraid you'll end our sessions and call me an asshole for the way I behaved after. For the way I haven't been able to get over it."

She gave me an encouraging smile, nothing but sincerity in her rich brown eyes. She was my age, and if I pretended hard enough, I could imagine we were just two old friends sharing our darkest secrets over coffee.

"You know I would never," she said, and I nodded.

Okay then, here goes nothing.

"Jim and I broke up senior year of high school," I said, and a lump formed in my throat as I thought about the memory. I had to force myself to talk and breathe around it. "My father gave us an ultimatum—his go-to of cutting me off and excluding me from the family if I didn't end things with Jim. I told Jim the truth, told him what my father threatened, and we both decided it would be better to take a break." I shook my head, hating looking back on that scared, weak little eighteen-year-old. Wishing like hell I could shake her and tell her the money didn't matter, the love did. The real kind of love, as young as it had been. Nothing had ever compared to it since.

"It broke my heart. Broke his too, I think," I said, swallowing hard. "But I held it together by telling myself that it would be a short break. That I would prove to my father that we were the real deal after graduation and everything would work out." I blew out a breath, my fingers shaking as the memory took hold. "Not long after, I went to a party the week of graduation," I said, shame coating me like a wet blanket. "I was with people who weren't really my friends, and my sister, who had begged and begged me to leave early. I'd already drank enough to wash away the pain of the breakup, and I was living in that moment of denial, the one where I never wanted the party to end." I wrung my hands out, trying to stop the tingling sensation I felt there with my rising panic.

"Sephie left," I continued. "Of course, she left. I told her to go. Told her I was fine and that I wanted to stay and dance some more. I wasn't fine, but I wasn't aware enough to realize that. I'd never drank that much before, but it was my first real taste at the sweet oblivion it could offer."

Dr. Casson nodded, quiet and contemplative as I spoke.

"There was a guy from our class, Kent Donnley, who started dancing and flirting with me. Bringing me more drinks."

Acid rolled in my stomach at the memory of his face, of

Kent's hands on my body. I could picture him as crystal clear as if he were in the room with us right now. *Him*, and yet I couldn't remember what some of my ex-husbands looked like thanks to the alcohol-induced marriages they'd been.

"I thought he liked me," I said, rolling my eyes. "I thought he was actually interested in me. I mean, he'd spent the whole night talking and drinking and dancing with me. And it felt good, to be paid attention to after I'd been forced to break up with Jim. After we'd both decided we'd be better off taking a break. I hate to admit it, but I'd wanted Jim to fight it. Wanted him to say 'fuck your father' and ask me to run away with him, but he didn't. He was so...supportive in that way I loved about him." I sighed. "Anyway, it felt good to feel..."

"Like someone thought you might be worth fighting for?" she asked.

"Yes," I said. "As ridiculous as that sounds."

"It's not ridiculous," she said. "It's human."

My eyes trailed to the side, tears crawling up my throat as I fell further into the memory, telling my story on autopilot as I tried to get the words out.

"You look just like her," Kent said after he'd brought me to his room to show me his football trophies.

I stumbled, barely catching myself on the wall to stay standing. It was super dark in here.

"Can you turn on some more lights?" I asked, my head spinning. "How am I supposed to see your trophies if it's so dark in here?" I asked when he didn't say anything. There was a lone lamp on across the room, not fully lighting up the space.

"If it's too bright we won't be able to pretend, and I know you want to pretend with me, don't you?"

I scrunched my brow, finishing the drink in my hand. I couldn't even really taste what was in the cup anymore.

"Pretend?" I asked.

"Yeah," he said, coming to stand in front of me, taking the

empty cup out of my hand and setting it down on the desk next to me.

He smoothed a hand over my cheek, the touch cold and empty as he inched his lips toward mine.

I let him kiss me, mostly because I was too slow to stop it. His lips met mine, hard and aggressive, nothing like Jim's. There was no care, no tenderness, no thought about what I liked at all. It was just...for him.

"Hey," I said when his hands started roaming over my body. "I don't—"

"Shh," he said over me, touching me everywhere. "You said you liked me."

Did I? I couldn't remember—

"You look so much like her tonight," he said. "If I ask really nice, will you let me call you by her name?" he mumbled against my neck, kissing and groping.

Ice encased my body, my sluggish mind finally catching up with the situation.

"I've always wanted to be with her," he continued, his movements frantic, possessive. "But she's untouchable. Not you, though, right?"

"What are you talking about?" I asked, lifting my heavy arms, trying to push him off.

"Your sister," he said. "For tonight, you're Persephone. You're going to be her for me, right?"

Cold dread filled my gut, my stomach plummeting to the floor. He tugged me toward the bed as my mind fully shut down...

Tears rolled down my cheeks as I finished telling her what happened, my body trembling with anger and shame and panic. "The next morning, when my mind was clear, I asked him how he was able to do what he did. He acted confused, arrogant even. Told me that I never said *no*."

Dr. Casson inhaled sharply, but managed to breathe out

slowly. She gripped her pen a bit harder, but her voice was even when she asked, "Did you file a report?"

"Heavens no," I said, rubbing my arms to try and bring life back into my body. I was wearing a warm sweater and slacks, but every inch of me felt cold. "I *didn't* say no," I said. "I shut down. It was like an automatic response when it came to people wanting me to be my sister." I hugged myself, unable to stop shaking. "I was an idiot. I should've fought harder, should've screamed and raged. I should've done anything but shut down." I shook my head. "All that time Jim and I were waiting. I shouldn't have waited. Kent stole that from me, but I let him."

"It wasn't your fault," she said, firm and supportive. "*Anne.*" The intensity in her voice had me focusing on her as she crossed the room, plopping in the chair right next to me. She reached out, taking my trembling hands in hers. "It wasn't your fault," she said again, and it cracked open some dam inside me.

Tears streamed down my cheeks, my body jerking slightly from the sob that came out of me. She pulled me into a hug as I took a deep breath, trying like hell to get a hold of my emotions.

"You've blamed yourself for way too long," she said. "The fault is on him. He took advantage of you—"

"But I was drunk," I said. "And I didn't—"

"You could've been drunk, naked, and dancing on a table. That does *not* give anyone the right to do anything to you without your consent."

I held on to her a little harder before finally letting her go. I swiped at my face, slumping back in the chair. "I hate him," I admitted. "But I hated my family more because I couldn't tell them. The shame it would've brought to the VanDoren name would've been the worst thing to ever happen to them."

Dr. Casson furrowed her brow, holding onto my hands.

"That's how they made you feel," she said. "That you were the worst thing to ever happen to them."

I nodded. "My father especially. My mother sometimes."

"And your sister?"

A new wave of tears washed over me, but I held them back. "Never," I said. "She never did anything to make me feel like I was the bad sister, the bane of the family's existence."

"But after what happened, she became the reason behind the trauma."

"Yes," I admitted, swirls of guilt sloshing around my insides. "She had no idea why I started treating her the way I did. But after a lifetime of never adding up to her and then after what Kent did..." I shook my head. "I shifted everything to her."

Dr. Casson nodded. "That was a trauma response, Anne. So was the alcohol and the partying and losing yourself in marriage after marriage. Those were all ways of trying to cope with what happened without actually coping."

I sighed, a weight lifting off my chest at her words.

"They were the response, but not the resolution," she continued.

"Can I heal from this?" I asked honestly. "Or will I always be broken by it?"

"You can heal from it," she said, squeezing my hands. "Unloading this burden you've been carrying alone for years is the first step, and while you can't erase it, as much as I wish we could, you can resolve it."

"How?"

"By not blaming yourself," she said. "By understanding you didn't deserve what happened to you and knowing you're worthy of healthy relationships and love for who you are, which has nothing to do with your family or wealth or anything else."

I sucked in a long breath, suddenly feeling as weightless as if I stepped into a warm, deep pool. She wasn't chiding me for being too drunk and not fighting harder. She wasn't calling me an awful human being for taking it out on my sister for so many years or for trying to outrun and drown the memory with alcohol. She was just holding my hands and looking at me with complete understanding and hope.

Hope.

For *me*.

"Now," Dr. Casson said, scanning my face. "How are you feeling after finally talking about what happened?"

I took inventory of myself, taking my time to sort through all the emotions just like she taught me. "Honestly?" I asked, and she nodded. "Happy," I said, laughing a little and feeling all the more ridiculous for it. "Angry and a little sad, but happy."

She smiled at me. "That's understandable," she said. "Those are very common reactions once you give voice to the things that have been haunting you."

"I can't believe I've never told anyone until now."

"You've held onto it for so long which only gave it more power over you. You've taken the power back now."

"It feels like that," I said.

"Good. It will take time to heal from this, and we can continue to work on it as we go along, but I want you to know how incredibly proud I am of you for opening up. I know it could be hard, but you should consider sharing your story with the people you trust, just like you have me. That took courage."

I laughed and waved her off. "No one has ever called me courageous before."

"Well, I am," she said. "You're doing wonderful, Anne. And you should really take ownership of that."

I *was* doing good. Working on myself and at two jobs, making new connections and friendships I would've never allowed myself in the past. Living a life I could actually remember.

That was all me. It wasn't Jim or my family. Just me.

Everything else was a bonus.

The realization gave me a new sense of authority over my life I'd never felt before, and I basked in it as Dr. Casson and I parted ways. If I could do that...if I could manage to cleanse myself of the past and move forward with an active role in my own life, then what else could be possible?

* * *

Okay, the universe absolutely fucking hated me.

There was no other explanation, except maybe that Dr. Casson had a sick, twisted sense of humor and was pulling off the worst prank in history, because there was no way *Kent fucking Donnley* had just been sat in my section with a group of friends.

I knew he still lived here. I'd looked him up when I moved back to town. He worked for some corporation in Charleston, but kept home here in Sweet Water. Social media was both a blessing and a curse and chalked full of information about past abusers.

"You okay, Anne?" Lyla asked after she'd done her dinner rounds in the dining room, checking on how the customers liked their meal.

"Fine," I said, snapping to attention. "I'm fine."

"Are you sure?" she asked. "If you need a break just tell me."

"I'm good," I said, letting anger and the newfound freedom I'd earned from my session earlier today wash over me. "Thanks though," I said, winking at her as I sauntered over to my newest table.

He had no power over me anymore.

He was nothing.

And I was...well, I was a work in progress, but he sure as hell didn't need to know that.

"What can I get y'all?" I asked, pen and pad in hand, my spine straight and my chin tipped just slightly.

"Four mules," he said, his friends laughing at some joke I hadn't heard.

"Anything else?" I asked, practically vibrating with too many emotions to track, but I tried to all the same.

Anger, for sure.

Fear, definitely there.

Embarrassment? Wow, yep that was there too.

Embarrassed that I ever let this asshole have so much control of my life. Control he didn't have a clue he held. He probably didn't even recognize—

"Andromeda VanDoren?" he asked. "Is that you?" A wide smile stretched his lips, the sight looking all wrong stretched over his face. Oh sure, he was handsome and charming and all the bullshit that helped people like him get away with whatever they wanted. He likely had a bank account that helped him get out of trouble too.

I shrugged. "Is there anything else y'all want?"

"No way," he said. "I can't believe it's really you! Since when do you work here?"

Why the hell was he acting like we were old friends? Was he really so obtuse that he had no clue what he'd done to me?

"It's been ages," he said. "It's so great to see you. You look *good*." He prattled on, eying me up and down like I was nothing more than a piece of furniture to be appraised.

"I'll go get your drinks," I said instead of responding to a thing he said, stomping toward the bar and placing their order.

I was tempted to give the table to one of the other waitresses, but something in the back of my mind told me that would be cowardly. He had no power over me anymore, and I was working to ensure he never would again. And the asshole didn't even remember what he'd done to me, by the way he was acting, or he just didn't think what he'd done was wrong. I couldn't decide which was worse.

Either way, maybe this was the universe's way of testing me. Testing my sobriety and my strength.

Well, joke's on you, universe, because I'm so *not relapsing because of this douchebag. Nice try though, but it'll take more than that to break me.*

The realization of that fact sank into my bones, filling me with a rush of confidence and strength. So much so, I took their drinks to them with a classic sugary-sweet-southern smile on my face, and barely looked back as I went to check on my other tables.

The night flew by, thankfully with Kent and his friends leaving after only two rounds of drinks and no more attempts to talk to me, thanks to my ignoring his every question. By the time I clocked out and said goodnight to Lyla— who stayed later than anyone to help clean and prep for the next day—I was exhausted but jittery in a way that I knew I wouldn't be able to sleep right away. It had been a long day, not just with work but with the session with Dr. Casson and somehow seeing Kent too. Like what were the fucking odds?

I gathered my things, typing out a fast text to Jim before I could stop myself.

Me: Just getting off work. Wired. Want to hang?

I bit my lip, hope fluttering in my chest. Hanging out with him after the day I had felt like the best way to put an end to it, even if all we did was watch Netflix and eat snacks. Actually, that sounded like the best way to end *any* day—

"There she is!" a familiar voice rang out as I walked out of Lyla's, heading toward the back road where employees parked their cars. Everyone else had already gone home, so there shouldn't be anyone hanging around this area, but there were four *someones*.

One in particular that made every bone in my body lock up.

"We were waiting for you!" Kent hurried toward me, clearly drunk.

Serving him drinks had been one thing, but seeing him out here waiting for me was another thing entirely.

My phone buzzed in my hand.

Jim: I picked up a night shift or I would. Sorry.

Me: Lyla's. Hurry.

It was all I could text before Kent reached me, the smell of vodka coming off him so strong it turned my stomach.

"We're going to a club," he said. "And I want you to come."

"No," I said firmly, moving past him to get to my car. I had no idea if Jim would come, and honestly, I didn't know if I needed him to, but instinct had made me send the text. If he was on a night shift, he could already be patrolling the streets, and the idea of having him here smoothed some of the fear scraping up my spine.

"Oh, come on," Kent insisted, following me every step of the way to my car. He stopped me from opening the driver's side door, his friends hanging out on the sidewalk next to my car, laughing. "We had some good times, right?"

I gaped up at him. "Move."

"No, you should come out with us. It'll be fun, I promise. I'll buy you a drink."

Every nerve in my body twisted, adrenaline making my body shake.

"I don't drink," I said, the words half-proud, half-determined. I tried to open my car door, but he wouldn't move.

"More for us then," he said. "Call up some of your friends. Maybe your sister? It'll be like a reunion."

I glared at him, but my instincts were screaming at me to run.

Okay, then.

I spun on my heels, heading around my car and back toward Lyla's. She was still inside, I could stay with her until—

He grabbed my arm, tugging me backward. "Don't go," he said, his words slurred.

"Don't touch me." I jerked my arm away from him, my entire body revolting at the feel of his hand on my skin.

"Easy," he said. "I'm just trying to convince you to come out with us."

"I don't want to!" I practically screamed the words. "Are you so dense that you can't understand that?"

His friends hissed, and I saw the shift from amused to angry in an instant.

Shit. Shit. Shit.

I walked backward, not wanting to take my eyes off of him while I tried to get to the back door. I'd locked it behind me, but Lyla would hear me. She'd let me in.

"Don't be such a pretentious bitch," he said, his friends laughing and clapping behind him. "I just wanted us to have some fun."

"No, you wanted to get your way and now that you aren't you're being an asshole about it. Leave. Now."

"Or what?" he snapped, stalking after me. "You're going to go tell your boss? What is she, five-five? She's not going to do a thing about us." His voice was lowered as he motioned to the dark, empty area around us with nothing but him and his friends around.

"Take one more step toward me and I'll claw your goddamn throat open," I said, my entire body shaking. I was six feet away from the door, but instinct screamed if I ran, he'd tackle me. I wasn't about to let that happen.

He took the step, and I lashed out, slapping him so hard his head snapped to the left.

"Oh," he said, a warning to his tone. "You're going to regret that."

"No, I won't," I said, defiant. He was like so many of my exes—arrogant, selfish, violent, and entitled. So many men like him prided themselves on being masculine and dominant when they were the furthest thing from it. Insecure and self-absorbed and controlling was more like it.

I drew my hand back in a warning as he crept toward me—

Red and blue lights flashed brightly, illuminating the scene. Relief barreled through me so forcefully my knees almost buckled.

"Step away from her," Jim's voice rang out with perfect authority as he got out of his patrol car. He shined a flashlight on the scene, stopping on Kent's face.

Kent raised a hand to block the light, taking a couple steps away. "We're just catching up, officer," he said. "We're good."

"No, we're not," I said, tears welling in my eyes. "He wouldn't let me get to my car. He wouldn't let me leave."

Jim said something into his radio, then headed toward me. All business, he stood next to me and kept his focus on the group of men across from me when all I wanted to do was fall into his arms. Dramatic? Sure, but *damn it* I was exhausted.

"You were holding her against her will?" Jim asked, then raised his hand toward the group of approaching friends. "I need you three to stand in a line on the sidewalk."

"Or what?" one of them snapped. "We're not doing anything wrong."

"Or I arrest you for interfering with an investigation," Jim snapped. "And keep your hands where I can see them."

They stood on the sidewalk, arms hanging by their sides.

"I wasn't holding her against her will," Kent said, lying through his damn teeth. "We were catching up—"

"How much have you had to drink tonight?" Jim asked, placing himself between Kent and me.

"A few," Kent said, all confidence as he raised his arms. "That's not a crime. And you don't see me driving. You've got nothing to hold me on."

Another patrol car pulled up, and Tanner stepped out. Jim filled him in, and Tanner headed to question and keep an eye on the three on the sidewalk.

Jim glanced at me, reading something on my face that made his eyes narrow. "He wouldn't let you get in your car?"

"No," I said. "He kept me from getting into it twice. Then he grabbed my arm when I tried to go back inside to Lyla's."

Anger flashed in Jim's eyes as he turned back toward Kent.

"I didn't! She's lying. Look, just let us go. We don't have time for this—"

"You should've thought of that before," Jim cut him off. "Place your hands behind your back."

"You're fucking joking," Kent said, shaking his head while Jim put him in cuffs. "You can't arrest me!"

"You're being detained for drunk and disorderly conduct," Jim said, continuing with his rights as he walked him to the back of his patrol car. Tanner let the other three go with a warning, and they practically bolted without a second glance for their friend.

Jim headed back to me after he got him secured in the car. "Are you okay?" he asked, none of the stern police officer to be found in his expression, just Jim.

"Yeah," I said, rubbing my arms. "I mean...physically," I admitted.

He reached between us, interlacing our fingers for a few precious seconds before Tanner called to him from his car.

"I have to go book him," he said, eyes curious and

concerned as he looked me over. "Do you want to come down to the station and make an official statement?"

"I..." My throat clogged, panic and fear strangling the words I wanted to say. "I can't." Making an *official* official statement would dredge up the past, leading to a trial that would no doubt drag the VanDoren name through the mud. I was doing everything I could to get back in my family's good graces, and this wouldn't be the way to do that.

I wondered if that mattered, though, in the grand scheme of things. He deserved to pay for what he'd done, but who was to say he'd done it to anyone else? Maybe it was just me. Maybe it was because of who I was and who I looked like. Maybe—

"It's all right," he said. "I can take a statement anywhere," he said. "Can I swing by once I have this done?"

"Please," I said, breathing out in relief. That would give me time to get my head on straight. Give me time to figure out the right thing to do. "I want to tell you something, when you come over."

"Of course," he said, squeezing my hand before walking me to my car. "I'll text before I head over." He opened my car door for me, ensuring I was safely inside before he gave me a reassuring smile and shut the door.

Safe. Jim made me feel so damn safe.

And after what I just confronted? Safe is the last thing I should feel, but it was impossible to deny.

I might be healing myself and my past, but Jim Harlowe was acting as my safe place to do that hard work, and I couldn't deny it one second longer.

I was in love with him.

I always had been.

And I didn't want to waste one more second denying it.

CHAPTER 12

Jim

"And that's the whole story," Anne said, tears streaking down her cheeks.

Acid rolled in my stomach, my world tipping on its axis as I listened to her tell me about her past, about what happened right after we broke up, about what that asshole did to her and the spiral she understandably had after.

It wasn't just the asshole that made her run away from everything she'd ever known or make her disdain for her family grow. It was a culmination of so many things, the pieces all set up like dominoes poised to fall—what happened to her that night was just the tipping point.

"Anne," I said, unable to form a coherent response. Saying I was sorry wouldn't change the past and it sure as hell wouldn't help her now.

I scooted closer to her on the lone piece of furniture she had, a vintage-looking loveseat she'd scored at one of the local markets when she first moved in. Slowly, I wrapped an arm around her, gauging her response to see if she even wanted to be touched after digging up the past.

She leaned into my embrace, holding tight to me.

"You didn't deserve that," I said, stroking my fingers through her silken hair. "You didn't deserve any of it."

Her body shuddered as she let out another sob, shaking her head against my chest. "You think I would be done crying over this," she said, her tone angry and sad.

"You feel whatever you need to feel," I said, knowing I wasn't one to tell her that one day it would all be better.

I had no clue if it would be, and I'd never give her false hope. But there were truths I *could* tell her, so I shifted to look into her teary eyes.

"You're the strongest woman I've ever known," I said, cupping her cheeks and swiping away her tears with my thumbs. "But crying and feeling the pain doesn't make you weak, Anne. It makes you human. Asking for help doesn't make you weak, it makes you *human*."

Her family's expectations her entire life—being the first-born VanDoren—had given her a knee-jerk reaction to operate at inhuman levels and place unrealistic goals on herself. It was a source of strain for her and her sister even before the incident, because Persephone made living up to those expectations look so easy while Anne had to work at it.

"But I'm the one who ran straight to a bottle," she countered, sucking in a sharp breath. "I'm the one who chose to behave the way I did after everything. *That* makes me weak, makes me broken."

I shook my head, moving my hands from her face down her shoulders until I could take her hands in mine. "Everyone reacts differently to the kind of trauma you've endured," I explained, drawing on my history of being a police officer for years. "I've seen it countless times," I continued. "Things like this happen way too often. It's awful and gut-wrenching and you never know how the person is going to cope. But there is no *wrong* way. You simply had to go through the rough of it before you could get to where you are now. There is nothing wrong with that."

A small, sad sort of smile shaped her lips as she met my eyes. "You're too good to me," she said. "You always have been."

"I'm just me," I said. "And I'd never be able to treat you any other way than you deserve."

A sigh slipped past her lips, like unloading the story for me had been another weight lifted off her chest. I was honored she trusted me enough with something she'd kept buried for years, but I still couldn't shake the instinct to head back to the station and pummel the piece of shit.

I'd locked him up in the drunk tank and filled out all the necessary paperwork before heading straight to Anne's. I wasn't in uniform anymore, but I was fucking tempted to head back there regardless of not being on duty.

But that's not what she needed right now.

"There have been several other times I've tried this, you know," she said, and I furrowed my brow, trying to follow her train of thought. "Sobriety," she explained. "There were so many bottoms I hit. So many experiences where I'd wake up and not remember where I was or I'd find a text I sent to my sister or family when I was drunk." She shook her head. "Something like that would happen, and I'd straighten up for a couple weeks. I'd tell myself I was stronger than this, tell myself that I didn't need to self-medicate anymore. That everything in my past had no power over me."

I held her hand, stroking my thumb over the top of it while she spoke, wishing like hell I had the right words to comfort her. "What changed this time?"

Anne visibly swallowed. "You'd think it would be the doctors telling me I'd die if I kept it up," she said. "But it wasn't."

The reality of her liver's condition sent waves of ice over my skin. The thought of losing her...

Fuck, it was unfathomable. I thought losing her all those years ago was bad, but at least I'd known she was out existing in the world, living her life in whatever way she chose. What if she hadn't come home? What if she hadn't gotten help? What if...

What if I never got the chance to tell her how I felt about her, even now, all these years later?

"Then what was it?" I asked gently, instead of dropping to my knees and begging her to see her worth, to understand how loved she was, how needed she was in so many people's lives, whether she believed it or not. That would be a selfish move, and I couldn't be selfish with her.

"When I couldn't even test to see if I could be a donor to save my mother," she said, squeezing my hand tighter. "That was the moment I realized I wasn't useful to anyone in any capacity."

A protest was on the tip of my tongue, but I kept my lips pressed together, not wanting to interrupt her.

"And it was an awakening," she continued. "Death was scary, sure. But the idea of leaving this world and it being a relief to everyone around me?" she shook her head. "That was an awful truth I had to face. Because yes, my family would grieve, but they would also probably be relieved they no longer had to try and fix me."

I parted my lips, anger flushing through me.

"*But*," she hurried on, noting my expression. "That was the moment I decided to see exactly what was broken inside me that needed fixing. That's when I finally acknowledged that the life I was living wasn't worth it, and that I needed to make a massive change if I wanted to make use of what life I have left." She smiled at me. "It's not easy, but this time, with

Dr. Casson's help...I'm learning how to cope. I'm learning more about myself than I ever have before."

"Good," I said, nodding. "That's really good, Anne. Because you absolutely are necessary in this world."

She huffed a laugh, the tone very much like she didn't believe me.

"You are," I pushed. "You may not believe it now, but someday you'll see how damn important you are in people's lives and that not every decision you make has to be to please your family."

Fuck, that last part I should've left out but I couldn't help it. Her father's unrealistic expectations of her had a huge hand in the way her life had gone, and I hoped one day he would take ownership of that.

"Thank you for listening," she said. "For coming when I texted. For understanding." She wrapped her arms around me, and I held her to me, just basking in the feel of her as she took all the time she needed to breathe. "I know I have no right to ask," she said after a few moments. "But could you stay tonight?"

"Yeah," I said, my voice cracking a bit. "I can do that."

Her tense muscles melted at my answer, and we headed to her bedroom. The mattress was small and on the floor, but it didn't matter. I held her through the night, doing my best to give her whatever energy I had, whatever she needed to help get through the aftereffects of revealing the truths she had tonight.

I didn't kiss her, even though I thought about it over a dozen times. She needed to be protected tonight, comforted and understood, not seduced.

She needed to be loved.

And even though a decade had passed, I loved her as much now as I did back then. Maybe even more. But I had no clue if it would be enough.

* * *

Early morning light filtered through the slats of Anne's bedroom window, falling over her sleeping face in strips of gold.

Fuck, she was gorgeous. Her long hair splayed over the pillow, her face relaxed after the intense and hard night she'd had last night. I didn't want to leave. I wanted to stay in that bed with her all damn day.

But I couldn't.

There was something I had to do before we both needed to go to work.

I gave her one last look, my heart filling too big for my chest, and headed to her kitchen. I'd ordered her favorite coffee and breakfast, and left it on the counter with a note explaining where I went. Her alarm would go off in ten minutes, and I didn't want her to feel alone.

Making my way to the station, I bypassed my coworkers and headed straight to the drunk tank. He was right where I'd left him last night, but the sight of him today? After knowing what I knew?

I wanted to fucking kill him.

I cracked my neck, my hands curling into fists as I headed into the tank. And just my luck, this asshole was alone.

"Finally gonna let me out?" Kent groaned as I stood over where he lay curled in a ball on the small bench in the room.

"After we have a little chat," I said, reaching down and grabbing him by his shirt, hauling him off the bench and across the room.

"Whoa, man, what the hell?"

I slammed him into the wall a little too hard, and I did my best to get a lock on my anger, but I didn't let him go.

"What the fuck did I do?" he snapped, trying like hell to shake off my hold.

129

He couldn't.

"You know what you did." I shoved him into the wall again, the line between professionalism and vigilante justice blurring for me.

"I was drunk last night," he said, like that was an excuse. "I said I was sorry when you chucked me in here."

"Not last night, asshole," I practically growled. "Ten years ago. At your grad party."

His brow furrowed, eyes lilting to the side like he was trying to remember.

"Anne," I said.

Recognition dawned in his eyes, and he fucking laughed. "Andromeda?" he asked. "You're pissed cause I fucked your girlfriend ten years ago?"

I yanked him off the wall, then shoved him right back into it so hard he groaned. "You didn't fuck her," I said, seething. "You took advantage of her."

"It was ten years ago, man. I can barely remember it." He gaped at me. "But we were partying," he snapped. "She didn't say no—"

I saw red and sank my fist into his gut.

He doubled over, and I had to take a step back.

"She didn't," he groaned, holding his stomach as he looked up at me. "She—"

I yanked him up by his shirt again. "She shouldn't have had to, you pathetic piece of shit."

"Okay, okay," he said, throwing his hands up in defense. "I swear I thought she was into it."

Disgust washed over me, twisting my gut. How many other girls had he said the same thing about? Anne didn't want to press charges because she didn't want a trial that was her word against his, but that didn't mean I couldn't dig into his past and see what I could find.

"I'm going to have your badge for this," he said once he could stand up straight. "You'll fucking regret this."

"Regret this?" I dragged him closer, letting him see every inch of my rage. "Try me asshole. I'll dig up every single piece of your past, which judging from the look of you, is likely littered with shit you've had to buy your way out of."

All the color drained from his face, and he looked close to pissing his pants.

"You take one step out of line, and I'll end you. You ever come near Anne again," I continued. "And I'll *forget* that I wear this badge."

He visibly swallowed, sheer terror shaping his features. "You her boyfriend or something?"

"Yes," I answered even though I didn't know what I was to her, but it went beyond labels for me.

Fear flashed through his eyes.

Good.

He should be afraid of me.

"I understand," he said, almost shaking where I held him now. "I haven't...I won't step out of line. Just leave me alone."

I released him, and he stumbled back against the wall.

"Good," I said, my fingers trembling with adrenaline. "Now get the fuck out of my station before I find a legitimate reason to keep you here forever."

He gave me a wide berth as he exited the tank, heading straight into Tanner who already told me he would do his out processing.

I didn't spare him a second glance as I headed past them and toward the back of the station where the training room was. We still had an hour before the new hires would report, and that would give Tanner plenty of time to get the prick out of here before Anne showed up.

But it wasn't enough to stop the adrenaline coursing through my veins.

Even hours later, I couldn't stop thinking about how I wanted to ruin the guy. And fuck, I'd been in uniform too. I could've lost my job if anyone felt the need to report my behavior, not that Tanner ever would. He was a good friend and an even better cop. He trusted me enough to know I wouldn't go off for no reason, and besides, it's not like I'd drawn blood.

I wanted to, but I managed to avoid that.

Anne had shown up to work looking amazing, no signs of the events of last night affecting her at all. The woman knew how to don a society-approved mask, and I wondered if that had helped her pain and struggles stay hidden all these years. If no one could see past the perfectly unaffected exterior she'd been raised to show the world, then no one could help her.

But I could see it. I could see it in the weight in her eyes when she thought no one was looking. I could feel it when she would walk by me, her hand grazing mine or my shoulder, like she needed assurance I was still here, still with her.

I was, despite all the reasons we shouldn't.

And with every innocent touch, every genuine smile or surprised laugh I managed to earn from her, I was a goner. My defenses unraveling until there was nothing left but unrestrained need.

"If it's all right with you," I said after all the new hires had left and we were done working for the day. "I'd like to follow you home, make sure everything looks good."

I knew Kent was properly scared of me and wouldn't be stupid enough to track her down and seek retribution for my actions, but I wasn't going to take any chances.

Anne's eyebrows rose, but she nodded. "I'd appreciate that."

I nodded, following her out of the station and onto the road. The entire drive my body was a tangle of nerves, twisting and tightening the closer we got to her apartment. Not because of any fear of the douchebag, but because I didn't know how to move forward with her.

I wanted her, needed her, but like she'd said before, she was working on herself. The last thing I wanted to do was complicate it with whatever was happening between us, but I honestly didn't know if I could stay away from her anymore.

"All good?" she asked after I'd checked the small bank of apartments she lived in, making sure there was no sign of Kent or his car.

"All good," I said, lingering just outside her door.

She worried her bottom lip between her teeth, but didn't say any more, so I smiled at her and turned to leave.

"Jim," she said, stopping me.

"Yeah?" I asked, turning around to face her again.

Her eyes dropped to the ground. "Stay with me?"

Those three words punched my chest, accelerating my heart with all kinds of hope.

But reality was enough to keep it in check.

"How long?" I asked, unable to not voice the question.

She tilted her head, and I stepped closer to her, scanning the lines of her face. God, I couldn't look at her without feeling a sharp pang of undiluted need. This was the girl of my dreams, the once love of my life, the woman who inspired me, who made me laugh, who understood me in a way that no one else did.

"How long can we keep doing this?" I clarified.

Understanding churned in her eyes. "Could we just take it one day at a time?" she asked. "That's kind of how I'm having to live my life right now. And I'm not certain of many things, like if I'll ever be fully healed or if I'll ever make up for my past sins, but there is one thing I know without any doubt..."

"What is it?" I asked, the tension between us tightening like a stretched string.

"You," she said. "I want you," she whispered. "In my life.

In whatever way you want to be in it. Friends, more than friends, anything. I'll take anything you want to give me, just please tell me you'll stay."

Her words broke me.

One second, I was a safe distance away, protecting both our hearts from the inevitable shatter that would happen when this all came crashing down.

The next, she was in my arms, my mouth over hers as I lifted her off her feet and carried her into her apartment, kicking the door shut behind me. I spun her, pressing her back against the closed door, taking her mouth in sweeping kisses.

"One day at a time," I echoed her sentiment against her lips.

"That's all we need," she said, her fingers frantic at the hem of my shirt.

I hauled it off with one hand, making quick work of hers next, then her pants and mine, leaving us in nothing but our underwear.

"Fuck," I groaned, backing up enough to appreciate her. She wore matching dark purple lace, the flimsy fabric clinging to her curves in all the right places. "You're beautiful," I said, claiming her mouth again as I cupped her breasts, teasing her nipples over the lace.

"James," she sighed against my mouth, arching into every touch.

I worked my lips down her neck, over the globes of her breasts, and lower, kissing her hips until I made it to my knees before her.

She looked down at me as I hooked my fingers into the edges of the lace, her eyes lust starved and lips swollen from my kiss. Slowly, I dragged the lace down her legs, my cock aching as she quickly stepped out of it.

"Look at you," I said, eyes flashing up to her and back to what was right in front of me. "All slick and needy for me." I slid a finger through her heat, and she gasped, rocking into the too-light touch. "So fucking responsive," I growled, gripping her hip with one hand while I teased her with the other.

"*James*," she groaned, her head back against the door, a hand tangling in my hair as I worked her, teasing her around the swollen little nub before pulling my hand away.

"You want my mouth, baby?" I asked, knowing full well she did. I just was dying to hear her say it.

"Yes," she said, breathless. "Please."

"How could I resist those manners?" I asked, shifting on my knees in front of her, drawing one leg up to rest over my shoulder so I had the perfect angle to lick her.

And I did.

In long, slow laps that had her entire body clenching with need.

Fucking hell, my cock was so hard it almost hurt. She tasted so fucking sweet and felt so damn good wrapped around my face like this. I could stay here all damn night and not get enough.

I swirled my tongue over her clit before dragging it down and plunging into her heat. Over and over again, I ate at her, feasted on her, lost myself in her until her thighs tightened and her breaths came in fast rushes, her fingers gripping my hair so tightly it sent ripples of delightful pain right down my spine.

"*James*," she said on a gasped breath. "I'm—"

I flattened my tongue, rocking it over her clit with the pressure she needed.

She exploded, her flavor bursting on my tongue as she came, her entire body trembling as she jerked against me. I held onto her hips, keeping her steady as I lapped at her until her body relaxed.

I pulled back, licking my lips as I carefully removed her leg from my shoulder so I could stand up.

Her blue eyes were half open, a smile on her face as she caught her breath.

"So. Damn. Beautiful."

"That was," she said, shaking her head. "You are…"

I grinned at the way she couldn't find her words. "Just getting started," I said before hauling her over my shoulder and carrying her to her bedroom. She laughed at the barbaric move, the sound only making me want her that much more.

"On your stomach," I demanded one I laid her on the bed, and *goddamn*, she flipped right over. "Good girl," I said, before smoothing my hand over the perfect globes of her ass. "Hips up," I said, grabbing two pillows and tucking them beneath her so that sweet ass was on full display for me, her breasts pressed against the mattress.

I dragged my hands over her back, relishing the chills that rose in the wake of my touch before I gripped her hips, shifting one of her legs to bend slightly while leaving the other one straight. Leaning over, I teased her slick pussy with my cock, groaning at how fucking soaked she was.

"Fuck," I groaned. "Condom?"

"I'm covered," she said. "Unless you want one."

I shuttered, a tremor rolling through me at the thought of taking her bare. We'd had the talk after our one-night-agreement which was now clearly blown to hell. We were both clean and had the tests to prove it.

"Are you sure, baby?" I asked, dragging myself through her wetness again.

"Yes," she groaned.

"You want me to take you like this?" I teased her, relishing the way her body responded to every move.

"Yes!"

"Hands on the edge," I demanded, my mouth at her ear as I bent over her, rocking through her wetness in the biggest form of torture to us both.

She reached up, gripping the edge of her mattress, her face turned toward the side so she could see me.

"Omigod," she groaned as I dragged my cock through her slickness again and again, working her up as I took my time kissing her spine before raising up above her.

"Do you feel that?" I asked, thrusting against her for emphasis but keeping myself from sinking into her to draw out her need. "Do you feel how fucking on fire I am for you?"

"God, yes," she answered.

"You're all spread out and on display for me, baby." I gently gripped her hips, rocking her against me. "I've got full control," I said, maneuvering her this way and that, showing her exactly how submissive this position was for her. She trembled with each move, her body clenching with each tease I gave her. "All you have to do is let me take care of you." I glided through her again, my hard cock grinding against her clit.

"God," she groaned, gripping the mattress tighter. "James." My name was a plea that sent primal pride zapping down my spine.

"You want to me to make you come on my cock?" I asked, my voice rough and low.

"Now," she said. "Make me come now."

Fuck.

She was so trusting, so giving, so free for me.

Mine.

I shifted up, moving so my cock set poised at her entrance as I held onto her hips. "Say please."

"*Please!*"

I slammed home inside her, bottoming out before pulling back and doing it over again. She moaned with each thrust, completely at my mercy as I took her from behind. I rocked into her, the angle from the pillows letting me sink so much deeper inside her.

"Fuck, baby," I groaned as I pumped into her. "You feel so

fucking good." Her pussy fluttered around my cock, matching her shaken breaths. "Already?" I smirked, releasing one of her hips to slip my hand beneath her, my fingers rolling against her clit as I continued to thrust inside her. "Like this?"

"Yes, yes, yes," she said, turning her head into the mattress as she moaned, her pussy clenching around me as she came.

Fuck, it was so hot. Watching her unravel for me. Watching her trust me enough to take care of her. It almost had me coming right along with her, but I held out, slowing my pace as she rode that high.

I reclaimed her hips, dragging my pace out to a torturous level that had her entire body trembling.

"One more," I said, upping my pace without warning.

Her surprised little whimper of pleasure had every inch of me on fire. Everything narrowed to the feel of her body around mine, to the sounds she made as I pumped into her over and over again.

"I don't know if I can," she breathed the words, her voice laced with pleasure and need.

"You can, baby," I said. "Give me one more." I gently shifted her bent leg higher, the angle allowing me even more access. I looked down between us, the sight of where our bodies connected enough to make me fucking see stars.

"God, James," she moaned as I spread her wider, using every inch of my body to make hers sing.

"I love it when you call me that," I groaned, pumping into her. "You only do it when I have you like this, when you need me like this."

"That, oh god, keep doing that," she demanded when I moved back to her clit, working it in light circles as I slid in and out of her with my cock.

Each stroke was an awakening.

Each pleasured cry from her was my undoing.

I loved this girl. Then. Now. Always.

And I silently showed her with every careful touch, every worshipping move.

Her pussy clenched tighter around my cock, and I pressed down on her clit while I pistoned my hips into her.

I groaned as her orgasm ripped mine from me, heat snapping down my spine as I came so hard I blacked out for a few seconds.

I slowed down, our bodies trembling as we rode the last waves of pleasure crashing between us. I held myself up over her, kissing her back before gently pulling out and climbing off the bed. I was back in no time, cleaning us up before drawing the sheets over us, her turning on side to face me.

"That was…" Her smile took over whatever she was about to say, and I couldn't help but return it.

I brushed back her wild hair with my fingers, kissing her in a slow, almost lazy sort of way. We didn't need to rush. We didn't need to think about tomorrow. We just needed to be in the now.

And as she closed her eyes, blissful exhaustion settling over her, I realized I was completely content to do just that…quite possibly for the rest of forever.

CHAPTER 13

Anne

"Your levels are improving," the doctor said as he looked over my chart. "The meds are working and your efforts really are making a difference."

A sense of pride washed over me as I glanced over at my mother, who had insisted on coming with me to my visit today. She was finally cleared to resume normal activities and she'd leapt at the opportunity to spend some one-on-one time with me.

"Have you been experiencing any issues?" he asked, sitting my chart down on the counter next to him. "Fatigue? Pain?"

I swallowed hard, the instinct to lie front and center. It was so ingrained in me to push my feelings to the side, to hide any real emotion for fear of being ridiculed, but I managed to work past it.

"Only when I forget to eat or I overwork myself," I said, and the doctor nodded.

"That's normal," he said. "You've got to keep yourself fueled," he continued. "Low sodium, lean proteins, high fiber."

"All the good stuff," I said, smiling at him. "Got it."

He chuckled. "You can treat yourself," he said. "It's all about moderation. We just want to keep your blood sugars in check. Listening to your body is key."

"I understand," I said. "Thank you."

"I'll see you in a couple weeks," he said, heading toward the door. "You're looking incredibly well, Mrs. VanDoren," he said on his way out.

Mom grinned at me, following me out of the room and back to my car parked in the lot.

"I'm so proud of you, Andromeda," she said as she buckled herself into the passenger seat. She could've easily had one of the drivers take us to this appointment, but I'd asked if I could pick her up.

I was now used to paying for it on my own, and there was something satisfying about using what I'd been working so hard for. It was the same with my small but cozy apartment—I found myself taking better care with it now that I worked my butt off to live in it.

It was a humbling, eye-opening experience that I found myself wishing I'd had years ago. But hearing my mother say those words? It was hard to speak around the way my heart expanded in my chest.

"Thanks, Mom," I said, trying not to cry. Sweet heavens, it felt like that's all I'd been doing lately, either from happiness or digging up the past. I was going to have to buy tissues on bulk for Dr. Casson if we kept this up. "That's all I've ever wanted."

The sky was a slate gray with an overcast of clouds, the promise of a winter rain on the horizon as I navigated the road toward her house.

Her house, not mine. That was another clarification I'd made after this whole situation. Father may have kicked me out and forced me to stand on my own, but in doing so, he made me realize that the house I grew up in hardly felt like a home. Not at the fault of my mother or my sister, of course, but mainly because of *me*. I'd never been comfortable there, and working through my past, I realized there were few places I'd felt safe and comfortable enough to be just me.

One of those places was anywhere Jim was.

Heat stole through my veins at the memory of last night, and the night before that, and the night before that...

Heaven help me, it had been a week of taking it *one-day-at-a-time* with Jim, and if I wasn't at his house, he was at mine. We worked together, slept together, ate meals and binge-watched shows together. It was a new, settled, wonderful kind of life I wasn't sure I deserved, but I was damn sure working on being worthy of it.

"Really," Mom said as I made my way up the drive to the house, parking the car so I could get out and hug her. "I think you're doing so well," she continued as I rounded the car and wrapped my arms around her. "I've always been proud of you," she said as I released her. "I just didn't think you were living your best life."

My chest tightened, but I accepted the strain of her bringing up my past, and nodded. "I wasn't," I said. "And I'm really sorry what I put you through. What I put you all through," I said, glancing at the house like that would encompass my sister and father too.

I'd apologized to Mom a dozen times already, and she'd graciously accepted those apologies, but I doubted there would be a time I'd feel like I was done apologizing. I'd made a lot of mistakes with her, but we were growing past that, and it meant the world to me.

"I told you it's in the past, honey," she said, waving me off. "What matters now is you're taking care of yourself. You're healthy and clear and I love having my daughter back."

Her words sank into my heart, filling me with hope. "I'm going to keep working at it, every single day."

And I knew I'd have to, too. There were countless times I

wanted a drink in the past few weeks, countless times the craving would creep up the back of my throat and beg me to soothe it, but thanks to Dr. Casson, I'd learned how to redirect that compulsive behavior. It wasn't easy, but it was working.

"Have you decided if you'll spend Christmas with us?" she asked. "I've spoken to your father, or tried to. He's still..."

Irritation bubbled up in my chest, and I resisted the urge to roll my eyes. "Still stuck in the past?" I offered for her.

"That and well, he's worried. He won't admit it, but after everything that happened with me and my surgery, and then finding out that he was so close to losing you too..." She sighed, shaking her head. "He's not handling the situation well."

"He's really not," I said. "I know I'm in no position to deny him any request." Even though every new demand made our relationship that much more strained. "And I want to earn back his respect, but the way he treated Jim lost him all of mine."

Mom's eyebrows rose, shock flashing over her features at my tone.

I shrugged. "I'm done sugarcoating things, Mama," I said. "Honesty is where I'm at. I'm doing what he says because I know it's good for me too—most of the things anyway—but I don't exactly want to come around for Christmas if he's going to bad-mouth Jim again."

"So Jim and you are..."

Happiness fluttered through my body, a giddy sort of rush that made my days so much brighter. "Taking it one day at a time," I answered.

"But he's in your life," she said. "And he's important to you."

"He's always been important to me." I swallowed hard, the decade-old wound of losing him stinging. Life would've looked very different if I would've just told my father to go

143

fuck himself. Jim and I might be married with a baby or two. We'd never know now.

"I'm sorry your father has an expectation that is outdated," she said. "But he's told me you've been spending a lot of time with Brad as well?"

I huffed a laugh. "I have."

Mom waited for me to elaborate, but I didn't. Brad and I were friends, good friends actually, and Jim knew all about the random lunch dates we'd been having. So did my father, and he could assume whatever he wanted as long as he kept the demands off my back.

"All right then," she said, grinning. "I do hope you'll come to Christmas. Persephone will be at an away game with Cannon, of course. It would be nice to have some quality time with you."

My heart ached, wanting to give in to her request right here and now, but I needed time. And it was okay to need time, to set boundaries with the family that had never really made me feel at home in recent memory.

"I'll let you know soon," I said. I had a week until Christmas, I could think on it, weigh the rewards versus the risks—which were me and Father butting heads in a way we wouldn't recover from.

"Okay, dear," she said, hugging me again. "Thank you for spending time with me today. Say hi to Lyla for me, will you?" she asked as she headed up the front porch steps. "Tell her I'm going to order a half dozen of those pies of hers for the holiday."

"Will do," I said, waving to her as I got back in my car.

I'd had to skip out of volunteer work today because of my doctor's appointment, which Jim totally understood, but I had plenty of time to make it to my shift at Lyla's, and Brad was meeting me there early for a late lunch.

. . .

"You aren't due here for another two hours," Lyla said when I walked in in full uniform.

"I have a late lunch date," I said, motioning to Brad who sat at one of the two-tops in the back of the restaurant.

Lyla laughed, her hair tucked up tight in a top-knot. "I think you just like me too much," she said. "It's like you live here with how many shifts you've been picking up."

Money was not an endless thing, I'd recently learned, and more shifts meant more security. "You're just that great of a boss," I said, and I really meant it. She was firm, damn good at what she did, but also probably one of the nicest people I'd ever met.

"Maybe I should be meaner," she said, winking at me as she headed back toward the kitchen. "Ensure that you take some time for yourself every now and then."

"You wouldn't dare," I teased. "Besides, I don't think you have a mean bone in your body."

"That's because you're on my good side," she said, laughing as she disappeared into the kitchen.

I highly doubted she had a bad side, but if she did, lord help the person who got on it.

"How's work treating you?" I asked Brad once I sat down and ordered lunch.

"Going well," he said.

"What is it you do again?" I asked, sipping my iced tea.

Brad laughed, shaking his head. "It's not that complicated. I'm an investor."

"For like a dozen different things," I said. "How am I supposed to remember all that? Let alone understand it."

"I mainly invest in real estate," he said. "Flipping houses, estates, corporations, whatever I think is a good deal."

"That I got," I said. "But wasn't there a company or something you recently bought?"

He nodded. "I buy and sell companies sometimes too."

"What about products?" I asked because I honestly couldn't remember. We'd grown close over the last few weeks, but the way he made money would likely always be a little fuzzy to me. I mean, he didn't do any *one* thing so it was hard to grasp sometimes.

"I've had people reach out," he said, tearing into his chicken after the waitress set down our food. "But I haven't found that special line of product that I think could be a real money maker."

"And it's always about the money, right?" I asked.

"Not always," he said. "I mean, yes, I have to see something as profitable or there's no point investing in it. But, if I found something I really believed in, something I wanted to back because I believed in the business, then I would take on a little risk to do it."

"Makes sense," I said, smiling before taking another bite of salmon. "So work is good then," I said, circling back to the beginning of our conversation.

He laughed again. "Yes," he said. "And so is yours, I can see." He motioned with his fork to my uniform.

"It really is," I said. "I love it here."

Like, really, really loved it here. I could easily see myself being content to do just this forever. When I was young, all I wanted to do was travel and study different cultures, but I'd done quite a lot of that and now I felt content to just *be*. Besides, there was always the future for any more historical research endeavors I wanted to do, and I definitely would work on some charities with Sephie—we'd already talked about focusing efforts for those in need in Charleston—but that wasn't what drove me.

This place did.

This new life did.

I was happy to come to work at Lyla's, and I was happy to volunteer with Jim.

And I was even happier to go to bed with him every night.

So happy I could see myself asking him if he might want to—

One day at a time.

Right.

I stopped my fantastical thoughts in their tracks, knowing it was way too soon to even begin going down that path. I'd rushed into marriages before and they never ended well. That mainly had to do with my choice of men and the partying we'd done, but still.

"What are you up to the rest of the day?" I asked Brad after we'd finished our meals and it was almost time for my shift.

"I've managed to coax my best friend for a night out," he said, following me up to the counter where Lyla had just set out her tray of *try-me* desserts for dinner service.

"Oh, who is the mystery BFF?" I asked.

"That'd be me," a female said behind me, and I spun around to see...

"Luna!" I said, smiling at the owner of *Luna's Boutique.*

"How are you, Anne?" she asked, offering me a kind smile when she stopped next to Brad.

"Wait," he said. "How do you two know each other?"

"I made her sister's wedding dress," Luna said, then tilted her head at him. "Why?" she asked, nudging him. "You afraid I've told her all your dirty little secrets?"

I raised my eyebrows at him. "Brad has secrets?" I laughed.

Luna nodded exaggeratedly. "Big time," she said.

Brad jerked her into a side hug, shaking his head as he looked down at her. "If you tell, *I* tell," he said, cocking an eyebrow at her. "Remember that."

"You're a menace," she said, shoving him off, but there was a laughter in her eyes that was pretty hard to miss. "Are we heading out?"

"In just a second," Brad said. "I've got to try these samples."

Luna rolled her eyes as Brad ogled the plate of treats, trying to pick out the best one.

"How long have you known this one?" I asked, nodding to Brad.

"All my life," she said, shrugging.

"She's been stuck with me since we were ten," Brad explained.

I furrowed my brow, trying to remember if I'd ever seen her at any of the charity functions but coming up blank. I'd feel like a jerk if I'd somehow forgotten her—

"Family friends," he continued, still scanning the plate of samples. "Not the kind that went to your father's functions—"

"Thank Christ for that!" Luna cut him off, then flashed me an apologetic look. "Not that there would've been anything wrong with that," she hurried to say. "You and Persephone are a delight..." she stumbled with her words, but I just waved her off.

Brad laughed, shaking his head. "She's not one for crowds, events, or anything that puts her in the public eye," he explained. "Basically your run-of-the-mill, anti-social introvert. I practically had to beg her to go out with me tonight—"

"Thanks, Brad," she said, rolling her eyes.

"I get it," I said. "No worries. Trust me."

Luna breathed a sigh of relief, then elbowed Brad in the abdomen for good measure.

"What'd I say?" he asked, looking so bewildered I couldn't help but laugh.

The bell above the restaurant door chimed, and I watched Jim and Ridge walk inside, Jim smiling at me, and Ridge looking...well, like Ridge.

Lyla popped out of the kitchen with another tray of samples, just as Jim and Ridge made it to us.

Brad finally popped a sample into his mouth, transporting him directly to flavor bliss heaven, his eyes rolling back in his head before he focused on Lyla as she sat down the tray. "Marry me," he said. "Marry me right now."

Luna rolled her eyes, but took a calculated step away from the group.

Lyla laughed, shaking her head. "You're the third one to ask me that today," she said, motioning to the butter cake he just tried. "I swear I should rename that to *marry me* cake." She winked at Brad, then pointed to the chocolate pieces she'd just put out. "Try that one."

Brad did while I hugged Jim, and Ridge stood there glaring at their exchange like he was personally offended, either by the cake or by Brad, I couldn't tell. Luna didn't look far off from Ridge's mood, but Brad said she didn't like crowds and he was about to make her hit the town, so it was understandable.

"Yep," Brad said after taking the bite. "It stands. Marry me."

Ridge pushed unceremoniously between them, grunting as he looked down at Lyla. I didn't realize how much taller he was than her until he was standing directly next to her, looking down at her like she was the source of his perma-scowl.

"If you're done being proposed to by the suit, can I get my to-go order?" he asked, his tone gruff and short in that way of his.

I opened my mouth, ready to apologize on his behalf to my boss and friend, but Lyla just popped her hands on her hips, staring up at him like she wasn't affected by his attitude one bit.

"Let me guess," she said. "Southern chicken tacos with a side of slaw?"

149

Ridge only grunted in response.

Lyla shook her head. "One of these days you're going to try the rest of my food."

"Why, so I can propose to you like him?" Ridge asked, motioning to Brad without even looking at him. Brad didn't seem to care, too busy popping another sample into his mouth. I playfully smacked his hand away when he went for thirds.

Lyla batted her eyes at Ridge, folding her hands over her chest. "Oh, yes, that's exactly what I live for. It's why I became a chef, so I could seduce grumpy men like yourself into proposing to me. Would you *please* put me out of my misery, Ridge?"

Wow, the sarcasm was strong with this one and I was so here for it.

I laughed, and so did Jim and Brad. Even Luna grinned, but Ridge didn't even crack a smile. Still, something churned in those eyes of his, and Lyla shifted her weight just slightly, as if she was preparing for a sudden storm.

They held their charged stare down for a few more seconds before I couldn't stand it a second longer.

"I'll go grab your tacos," I said to Ridge, hooking my arm through Lyla's as we headed back to the kitchen.

"I have half a mind to skimp him on the slaw," Lyla said as she gathered up his order.

I laughed again. "He'd only come back and demand more."

"Insufferable," she said. "You know he came in here two nights ago, saying I didn't give him enough crema?"

"The nerve," I said.

"Exactly." She boxed up his order and handed it to me. "Would you please? I don't have the energy for him tonight."

"With pleasure," I said, giving her a reassuring smile as she busied herself with the first incoming orders of the dinner rush.

"Here," I said, handing Ridge his order. "Stop giving my friend a hard time."

He narrowed his gaze on me, then nodded to Jim as he headed out without another word.

"Eloquent as always," I said, and Jim laughed.

"That's Ridge," he said, shrugging. "Your friend already took off with the redhead," he continued.

"That's Luna," I said. "She owns the vintage shop down the road. She's the one who made my sister's wedding dress."

"Oh yeah," Jim said. "I've been in there a couple times, she's nice." He shrugged. "I think Brad knew if he stood here a second longer, he'd eat all the samples, so he dragged Luna out of here."

I plucked up a piece of the chocolate cake, and held it to Jim's mouth. "I mean, can you blame him?" I asked.

Jim took the offered treat into his mouth, his lips wrapping around my fingers for a split second. The action had a thrill shooting straight down the middle of me, and suddenly working my shift was the last thing I wanted to do.

"Oh, damn," he said after swallowing. "Yeah, I totally get it. I'm gonna go propose too." He moved past me, and I grabbed his arm, gaping at him.

He laughed, the sound grazing my bones and making me shiver. "What, you said she was super nice."

I playfully smacked his chest. "Jim Harlowe, don't you dare play with my heart like that."

He brought me in for a hug, nuzzling my neck like he needed all the attention in the world. "I wouldn't dream of it," he said, then poised his lips at the shell of my ear. "Besides, who needs cake when I have that sweet pussy waiting for my mouth?"

Red hot liquid slid through my veins. How could the

sweetest man on the earth have the absolutely dirtiest mouth? And why did it turn me into a puddle every single time?

"How am I supposed to work now?" I asked as he pulled away, all innocence and charm on his face.

"Find a way," he said, winking at me. "I'll see you at my place after?"

"Depends on how many more women you plan on proposing to before I get there," I teased.

* * *

By the time I helped close Lyla's and make it to Jim's place, I was half-dead on my feet.

Well, not literally because I was a good girl and followed the doctor's orders, making sure I took breaks, drank tons of water, and munched on healthy snacks between tables.

Now, I was hoping I could get *Jim* to call me his good girl because that really did do something to my damn brain chemistry. I could be a strong, independent woman during the day all I wanted, but come night time? I was more than ready to do anything and everything to get him to say those two little words. And the fact that he gave me the space to be both versions of that woman made me love him even more.

Not that I'd told him yet.

Because I was terrified of making things too serious too quickly.

One day at a time.

"You're here," Jim called as I let myself into his house. The man had already given me a key, and it felt like Christmas even though it was a week away.

"I'm here," I said, dropping my bag on the little table he had in his entryway. I kicked off my shoes, sighing in relief.

"Come back here," he called from what sounded like his back patio. "I have a surprise for you."

Excitement fluttered through me, hurrying my steps as I made my way through the kitchen and out the back door.

"Wow," I said, surveying the scene.

Flames flickered in the center of an outdoor table, sparkling gravel lining either side of the burner, casting everything in a rich, warm glow. A bottle of sparkling apple juice sat in a bucket of ice, two glasses beside it. Jim stood next to one of the cushioned patio chairs, a sheepish look on his face as he held something behind his back.

"What's the occasion?" I asked, practically brimming at the romantic scene.

"You're always the occasion," he continued. "But if you need a label, you can call this an early Christmas present."

I pressed my lips together, suddenly feeling out of the loop. "I don't have your gift here," I said. I had it at my house, wrapped and under my Charlie Brown tree.

"I don't need a gift in return," he said, shaking his head. "This was a spur of the moment type of thing and if you hate it, we can make other arrangements."

"Okay, now the suspense is killing me." I stepped closer to him, the warmth of the small flames chasing away the slight bite to the air. Christmas time in South Carolina was never freezing, but at night it could get cooler, so the fire was a nice touch. "What are you hiding back there?"

"Well—"

A very cranky *meow* sounded from behind him, and Jim cringed a little as he brought his hands in front of him.

Shock had me gaping at the black bundle clinging in his arms, the cat looking downright *pissed* to be there.

"*Surprise*," he said, worry coating his features.

"That's not the..." My voice trailed off as the cat wiggled awkwardly in Jim's arms.

"The same cat from the night I almost had to arrest you?" he asked, laughing as he struggled to hang on to the creature.

"Oh my goodness," I said, reaching between us to take it from him. "Where did you find him?" I asked, tucking the cat between my arms. "It is a *him* right?"

Jim nodded. "It's a him. And I never lost him," he explained. "I took him to the animal shelter, who adopted him out to Barbara."

"The elderly woman you check on every week?" I asked, my heart warming at how damn sweet he was. He never missed his Wednesday night check in with her.

"Right," he said. "But it turns out it wasn't such a great fit. He didn't get along with her dog Dane. It turns out this little beast only seems to calm down for you."

The beast was currently purring in my arms, his golden eyes almost shut as he settled into my hold. I tsked him, moving to sit down on one of the patio chairs. "I guess that's what happens when you go through extreme situations together," I teased. "We formed a bond among the chaos."

Jim laughed, taking a seat next to me. "He needed a home."

"You adopted him for me?" I stroked the little guy's fur, the vibrations from his purrs having a super calming effect on me.

"Yes," he said. "But I'm not expecting you to take care of him on your own," he hurried to explain. "I'm not giving you a task. I have everything he needs here, and I bought a duplicate set of supplies in case you wanted to keep him at your apartment."

I melted. Like seriously melted. I might be dripping right off the chair as we spoke.

"But if you don't want the responsibility, I can take care of him here for us. Just, when the animal shelter called, I couldn't say no. Not when he's the reason you came back to me." He reached over and timidly pet the sleeping bundle.

"Jim," I said, emotion clogging my throat. "This is the best present I've ever gotten."

Jim released a breath.

"He's perfect," I continued, leaning over to kiss Jim.

The cat protested in my arms, wiggling free and leaping out of my lap, darting straight in through the opened back door like he owned the place.

Jim laughed. "He already knows where his litter box is," he said, reaching over to the sparkling apple juice and pouring us two glasses. "And his tree scratch post thing and a bed. I don't know much about cats, I just got what the girl at the shop said."

I grinned so hard my cheeks hurt, taking a sip to try and hide just how big my smile was.

"Did you propose to her too?" I teased.

"Oh, you've got jokes, huh?" He took my glass, setting it and his down before he gently hauled me into his lap, showering me with kisses that made me laugh and arch into him at the same time.

"You're the one dreaming of whisking my boss off her feet for a never-ending supply of cake."

"I love it when you get all territorial," he said, his kisses growing longer, slower against my neck.

Warmth flushed my skin, and I shifted on his lap, settling one leg on either side of him. "Is that right?" I asked, rocking over what I could already feel was hard beneath me. Goodness, I'd never get enough of this intense need for each other. I kissed his lips, then the line of his jaw, before nipping at the lobe of his ear. "You like seeing me jealous, James?" I whispered, rolling my hips.

He groaned, hands flying to my hips and making me do it again as he captured my mouth. "I like anything that makes you look like *mine*."

A hot shiver raked my body at his words.

"I am," I said on a breath. "I am yours."

He went still beneath me, his eyes locking with mine. All jokes vanished, replaced with a primal intensity that made a white-hot knot form in my core.

"Say that again," he said, emphasizing his demand by dragging me over him again.

"I'm yours," I said, breathless as he moved me on him again and again, winding me up even though we were still fully dressed.

"Fuck," he groaned, kissing me hungrily. "Feel what you do to me?"

I shivered, reaching down between us, unzipping his pants so I could wrap my fingers around his cock. He thrust into my hand. "I feel that," I said, grinning as I kissed him again.

God, I could spend hours just kissing this man. It was the perfect balance of claiming and giving, thrilling, and as comforting as a warm blanket. He had a direct line to my bliss button, and sweet heavens did he know how to push it.

I stroked his considerable length in my hand, gripping and pumping while kissing him so intently I could barely catch my breath.

"Anne," he breathed my name between my lips, wrapping his arms around me as he stood up, taking me with him. He pulled back enough to catch my gaze, walking us into his house and shutting the door behind us.

We made it to his bedroom, where he gently laid me down on my back.

I waited for the sinful demands to spill from his lips, but none came. Instead, he took his time undressing the both of us, separating the actions with lingering kisses along every part of my body.

"I'm yours too, you know," he said as he gently nudged my thighs apart, settling himself between them. His face was above mine, our bodies aligned, his eyes seeing straight through to the heart of me.

This was different.

I could feel it in the shift in his kiss.

Could feel it in the gentle way he glided inside me, the way he took my body in long, slow strokes, his eyes on mine with every move so he could watch every ripple of pleasure cross my face.

This meant something.

And my heart soared at the silent communication, at the bond I felt growing between us with every passionate kiss, every gentle caress, every worshiping attention.

The words in my heart threatened to spill from my lips as Jim worked my body into a pliant spark of pure, undiluted pleasure.

I love you. I love you. I love you.

I wrapped my arms around him, drawing him even closer as we crashed against each other in slow, intentional waves.

He was everything and then some.

And for this blissful moment, I could pretend that nothing in the world would ever be powerful enough to separate us.

"James, I..." My words trailed off as he snaked an arm beneath my lower back, hauling me up against him as he ground against my clit while pumping inside me, sending me into absolute orbit.

"I've got you," he said, misinterpreting my words, thinking I was telling him I was going to come when in reality I was about to tell him I loved him.

But he *did* have me.

And his thrusts were like match strikes inside me, sending flames licking up and down my spine until I combusted.

I whimpered as my orgasm tore through me, so powerful I

convulsed around him, clinging to him through the intensity of it as he found his own release inside me.

He held me against him, rolling us to our sides as we lay there catching our breath.

And I knew that *this* was the life I'd always been waiting for.

Now all I had to do was manage to hang on to it.

CHAPTER 14

Jim

"I really appreciate you two meeting me here," I said as Cannon and Persephone took their seats across from me in the booth at Sweet Water's most popular bar *Scythe*. I had to pick a place I knew Anne wouldn't catch us, and fucking hell, my nerves were on high alert as her sister settled in next to Cannon. "I know your schedule is tight," I said, flashing Cannon an appreciative look.

"It's all good," Cannon said, wrapping an arm around Persephone. "Home game is tomorrow, then we're away at Christmas."

I nodded, taking a deep breath to try and get my words straight.

Persephone leaned a little over the table, bracing her hands on it like she needed it for support. "Please, Jim," she said, her voice severe. "Just be straight with us. How bad is it?"

I furrowed my brow. "What?"

"Is Anne struggling? Does she not want to tell me because she's afraid I'll tell our father? I won't—"

"Oh, shit, I'm so sorry," I said, not even once thinking that me asking them to meet me here would lead to those kinds of thoughts. "Anne is wonderful," I hurried to say. "Honestly. She's amazing."

Persephone released a sigh I think the whole bar heard, and there was more than a fair share of Reapers who casted glances our way, almost like it was a habit to check up on their own. She leaned back in the booth, settling into Cannon's side a little more.

"I'm sorry," she said. "When you called, and then picked here to meet, I just…"

"It's my bad," I said when she didn't finish. "I picked here because I didn't want Anne to know we were meeting."

Cannon cocked a brow at me, narrowing his gaze as he scanned my features. Something clicked, and he let out a rough laugh. "Holy shit," he said, smiling down at his wife. "He's in love with her."

Persephone's mouth parted, surprise lighting her eyes.

"Is it that obvious?" I asked.

"Not at first," Cannon answered. "But I can see it."

"Is that why you called us here?" Persephone asked, a little excitement rising her tone.

"Yeah," I said, rubbing the back of my neck. "I was hoping I could get some advice." I eyed Cannon, who was the most recent addition to the VanDoren family. "Cannon, I know you mentioned you had some issues in the beginning with…Mr. VanDoren."

"Issues," Cannon said, huffing. "He hated me."

I blew out a breath, my shoulders dropping. "He's hated me for a decade," I said. "And you have an NHL contract, accolades, and millions in the bank. If you didn't have a chance, what kind do I have?"

"First off," Cannon said. "I've told you this before, *fuck* the money part of it. That shit shouldn't matter."

"I know that," I said. "But her father doesn't. No offense," I said to Persephone, who waved me off.

"You're not wrong," she said.

"How did you get in his good graces?" I asked Cannon.

"I don't entirely know if I am," he said. "We've come to an understanding, but I think it will be a long time before I have his full trust."

"I love her," I said the words, and the act of doing so out loud was a freeing and terrifying thing. "And I know she's working on healing. I know she has to focus on herself right now. I'm not trying to take that away from her. I don't want to be one of her rushed marriages, I just want her to know she's it for me and that I'll support her—"

"Omigod you're going to propose!" Persephone squealed, and half the bar looked over at us.

I laughed as Cannon smoothed his hand up and down her back. "Maybe a little louder next time, Princess," he said. "I don't think they heard you down at *Lyla's Place*."

Persephone covered her mouth, but bounced in her seat. "I'm just excited."

"I'm terrified," I admitted.

"When?" Persephone asked.

"After Christmas, when she finishes her volunteer work with me and has some time to take off. I was thinking we could get away for the weekend." Somewhere close enough she could still make her sessions with Dr. Casson but removed enough to feel like a treat.

"How romantic," Persephone said, sighing a little.

"Should I ask permission?" I asked the main question that was haunting me right now. I knew her father would be pissed if I bucked his traditions and didn't ask for his daughter's hand in marriage, but I also knew he would most likely say no even if I did try to do right by his standards.

"Yes," Cannon said at the same time Persephone said, "No."

"Well that clears that up," I said, leaning back in the booth.

"Wait, what?" Cannon gaped down at his wife. "You know the hell he gave me after what happened to us?"

"I most certainly do, Cannon Price," Persephone said, using a tone that made Cannon's eyes light up in a way that made me feel like I needed to vacate the booth right the fuck now. "But our situation was entirely different from theirs," she continued. "My father has been a horror to Jim since we were teenagers," she said, looking me dead in the eye. "He doesn't deserve the respect you're showing him."

My mouth dropped just a bit at her directness, but it also made me smile.

"But what if he threatens to disinherit her again," I said. "Like all those years ago. What if he uses everything in his power to pull us apart again?" I hated how pathetic it sounded, to be so afraid of an outside force holding control over my future, but how could I not? He'd done it once, he could again.

"What if Anne relapses?" Persephone asked, giving me whiplash. "What if the health of her liver plummets and she needs surgery? Will you still support her? Love her?"

"Of course, I will," I said, heart racing at just the thought of what she suggested happening.

"What if she falls into old habits, trying to push everyone away and flee across the country?"

"I'll chase after her," I said, determined. "I won't ever force her to be anyone other than who she is at her core. I won't force her to be with me, but if she wants me, I'm there. Nothing will keep me away."

A bright, satisfied smile shaped Persephone's lips as she glanced from me to her husband and back again. "Then fuck my father," she said, raising her glass of tea toward mine.

"Jesus," Cannon mumbled under his breath, raising his glass too.

My smile matched hers, realization clicking into place with her line of questioning. Nothing could keep me from loving her—not a relapse, not old habits, and certainly not her father.

I tapped my glass against theirs, my heart soaring at the newfound confidence.

"Thank you," I said, slipping out of the booth.

"He's going to lose his shit," Cannon grumbled, standing up to shake my hand. "You know that right?"

I nodded, shaking his hand. "I know."

I tried to release his hand, but he kept on shaking it. "She's doing better," he said. "When I met her she was...she was hurting. And now she looks healthy and happy. I know that has more to do with her than you, but keep it up."

"I will."

Cannon released my hand, giving me an approving look that meant more to me than any Anne's father could've offered me. Because Anne respected Cannon's opinion more than his anyway, and her sister's even more.

And with them in my corner, I felt like I could take on the world if I had to. I had their blessing, and in the end, that's all that mattered.

* * *

"Why are we here, Jim?" Ridge asked me a few hours later as he followed me into Luna's shop.

He followed me inside, practically on my heels as I headed straight for the small selection of jewelry the boutique offered. I'd already scoped out a few places in Charleston, but I hadn't found the right one yet.

"Are you going to pop the question?" Ridge asked. "Because you know I'd never marry a cop."

I laughed, shaking my head. "I think you would," I said. "Seeing how you rarely share your humorous side with anyone but me."

Ridge folded his arms over his chest, the motion putting his sleeved arms on display. "Why the fuck are we here?" he asked, sounding more like himself.

"I'm going to ask Anne to marry me," I said just as Luna walked up to the counter. We'd had a brief encounter at Lyla's Place before Brad practically dragged her out of there, so she knew I was with Anne.

"Oh my gosh, that's amazing. Congrats!" Luna said. "What can I show you?"

"Holy fuck, you're serious," Ridge said, eyes wide.

"Absolutely," I said, turning away from the rings for a moment. I needed my best friend to be with me on this, but if he objected...it wouldn't matter. I loved her. End of story.

He dropped his arms to his side, tilting his head back and forth before he grabbed me and crushed me in the quickest hug of the century. He clapped me on the back, then motioned an arm to the counter. "All right, then," he said. "Let's get these rings out."

Luna grinned at him before unlocking the glass display, her fiery red hair hanging in a long braid over her shoulder.

"I know Anne a little through her sister, and Brad has told me some things," she said. "But can you tell me a little bit more about her?"

"She's..." Fuck, how could I describe her? A smile spread across my face as I thought about the best way. "She's chaotic but solid, calm but feisty, and scary on the best of days. She's wild, funny, and brilliant. Independent but also knows when she needs help. She's..." My voice trailed off, and Ridge rolled his eyes.

"Fuck, you're so whipped," he teased.

"I feel the vibe," Luna said, nodding as she hunted through her case. "What do you think of this one?"

She pushed an opened velvet box toward me, the thing dusty on the top but sporting a ring inside a torn silk cover. The ring had a crown setting that sparkled with smaller diamonds, the larger diamond in the center solid black.

It screamed Anne—it had her royalty-like flair but also her unflinching uniqueness. It had her mystery, her wildness, everything.

"It's from the Victorian era," Luna continued, giving me more information even though I was already in love.

"I'll take it," I said before she could continue.

"Oh, wonderful," she said. "We can get it sized if it doesn't fit after she says yes." She winked at me. "I'll head over to the register and wrap this up for you."

After she said yes.

God, I hoped she said yes.

She might not. I mean, I would understand. She'd been married before. Several times. Who was to say she ever wanted to do that again?

Nerves threatened to steal all my newfound confidence away. Maybe I was rushing things. Maybe—

"Get out of your head," Ridge snapped, gripping my shoulder.

I blinked a few times, nodding. "Right."

"When are you asking?"

"A few days after Christmas."

Ridge nodded, motioning me toward where Luna was waiting for us. "You've got time then," he said. "Breathe."

A week.

I had a week until I planned to ask her, but honestly, if I felt for a second she wasn't ready, I wouldn't put that on her. I could feel her out. Make sure I wasn't going to cause her any kind of pressure or stress. I could buy this ring and hold onto it for however long I needed till the time was right.

But from the way we'd been living these past few weeks? Either at her place or mine, sharing the love of a chaotic little beast of a cat she'd named Binx?

I felt like *forever* was just a question away.

CHAPTER 15

Anne

"Anne, are you good to cover a few extra hours?" Lyla asked as I cleaned up in between the afternoon rush and dinner rush.

"Definitely," I said.

"You're a life saver," Lyla said, wrapping me in a quick hug. "Bonnie called in sick, and you know how the day after Christmas is."

"Totally get it," I said waving her off.

"I'll make it up to you," she said as she headed back to the kitchen. "I owe you dinner somewhere other than here already. One of these days we will get that girls' night."

"Keep telling yourself that, work-a-holic," I teased, holding my smile until she'd disappeared behind the kitchen door.

I let it drop once she was out of sight. I had no problem covering another shift tonight, I was just exhausted. Christmas with my parents had been...well, it wasn't awful but it wasn't a Norman Rockwell painting either. It had meant everything to see Mom so happy and to have a meal that just revolved around the three of us, but I couldn't exactly ignore the wedge between my father and myself.

He had been kind though, and even said he was proud of me, so that was something. And it was also something to realize that I no longer *needed* that approval or attention. It was a sad discovery, but a necessary one. I'd told Dr. Casson all about it this morning, and she'd helped me work through the sort of grief-like feeling that accompanied the realization that my worth wasn't dependent on my father's or any of my family's opinions anymore.

I was worthy of love.

I was worthy of happiness.

I was a good person doing my best to do good things.

The doc had me repeat this so many times I almost believed it. And maybe that attributed to my exhaustion today, but something in the back of my mind nagged at me that it was something else, I just couldn't put my finger on it.

After another hour of waiting tables, my head was fuzzy like I'd had a few drinks, but that definitely wasn't the case.

Shit, I'd forgot to eat today. *Again*. I didn't mean to, but it was a full day with a session with Dr. Casson and then my last day of volunteer work with Jim, quickly followed by a double shift here.

I was hungry, that was all. I'd get something once I closed out this table.

"Hey, stranger," Brad's voice filled the space behind me, and I whirled around with a smile.

"Hey there, how was your holiday?" I asked as he took up a lean at the front counter.

"Can't complain," he said. "That's why I'm here. I brought your present."

"You didn't have to," I said. "Give me a minute though, I need to get them drinks." I motioned to my table, indicating to Brad that I'd be right back.

I went to grab my table's drinks, piling them on the tray at the drink station when a searing, sharp pain sliced through my side.

I yelped so loud Lyla came running out of the kitchen, and Brad hurried around the counter toward me.

"Anne?" Brad asked.

His voice sounded far away, my head suddenly swimming like it was trying to get away from the pain.

Another wave crashed over me, and I dropped the tray, the glasses plummeting to the floor in a loud shatter. I grabbed my side, black dots splashing across my vision.

"Anne!" Lyla yelled, then said something to Brad I couldn't understand.

Wait, where was I again? And why was Brad reaching for me?

Heaviness and confusion sank over me, pulling me down, down, down—

My legs gave out, and I fell against someone, darkness fully washing over my eyes, sweeping me away until all I could hear was static.

CHAPTER 16

Jim

ME: You working later than planned?

I typed out the fast text with one hand and pet Binx with the other. He'd finally, officially warmed up to me once he realized I wasn't going to force him out on the streets again.

Plus, I bribed the guy with tuna twice a week, so it was hard for him to stay mad at me for long.

Anne was running late, but I figured she was just caught up chatting with Lyla. She'd become a good friend and boss—

Lyla's number flashed across my screen before I'd even put my phone down, and some buried instinct in me woke up and stood at attention.

"Lyla?" I asked by way of answer.

"Hey, Jim," she said, and the tone of her voice had my stomach plummeting. I knew that voice. I had to use that voice all the time relaying difficult news to people after car accidents or something equally terrible.

"What's wrong?" I was already standing, grabbing my keys off the drop station near my front door.

"Anne's okay," she said, but the tone of her voice didn't

give me an ounce of comfort. She sounded like she'd been crying. "She is. We're at the hospital now—"

My entire world shifted on its axis, and I slipped into the kind of shocked calm that came with my profession.

"What happened?" I asked as I climbed into my car.

"I'm not exactly sure," she said. "She had an episode at work and then she passed out."

I cringed against the image she painted in my mind, and hurried onto the highway.

"They rushed her back," she continued. "Brad was at my restaurant. He caught her before she could hit her head when she blacked out. And he called her family on the way over. I'm sorry, I didn't think to call you until we got here. I feel awful, but it all happened so fast."

"You did everything right," I said, assuring her. "I'm on my way," I said. "Thank you for calling me." We hung up, and I broke speed limits to get to the hospital. Tanner was on duty tonight so I knew I was in no danger of getting pulled over.

I made it there in record time, barely registering where I parked before I raced inside, spotting Lyla in the lobby.

"She's on level three," she said. "I was just coming down to wait for you."

"Thank you," I said, barely stopping to speak as I raced up the stairs. Fuck the elevator, it would take too long. I wasn't sure if Lyla was behind me or not, but I didn't stop as I cleared the third floor, rounding the corner toward the reception check in, bypassing it and smacking directly into Mr. VanDoren's back.

"I'm sorry," I said, righting myself and trying to catch my breath. "Where is she? Is she all right? What are her levels at?" The line of questions came out in one panicked string.

"What the hell are you doing here?" Mr. VanDoren grumbled, but Anne's mother stepped around him, pushing him back with nothing more than a look.

"She's in room three-thirteen," she said. "She's stable, but still unconscious. Her liver levels spiked, and the doctor said some fluid had accumulated there and caused an infection that had some instant affects."

"How?" I asked, a small amount of relief slipping air into my tight lungs. She was okay. She was stable. It would be all right. Anne would be all right.

"*How*?" Mr. VanDoren snapped, moving around Mrs. VanDoren. "How? Probably from overworking herself at your department." He glared at me. "Hell, you probably even convinced her to go to one of those cop bars after work, didn't you? Did you pressure her into drinking again? Did you—"

"Hell no," I cut over him, anger snapping through my veins. "I would never put her well-being in jeopardy."

He looked at me like he didn't buy it for a second. "You've never cared about her well-being—"

"Here are those coffees," Brad's voice cut over Mr. VanDoren's tantrum as he came around the corner, holding two white cups in his hands.

Anne's parents took them from him, and I knew he was a good guy but goddamn he was making it hard to like him right now. I mean, fuck me, the guy was there when Anne passed out. He had been there to catch her. And Mr. VanDoren looked at him like he was the son he never had.

"Thank you, *Brad*," he said, shooting his name at me like a bullet. "It's wonderful to have someone here who actually cares about Andromeda's future."

Brad furrowed his brow, instantly taking a step away from Mr. VanDoren like he could separate himself from the death glare he was giving me.

"Anne's my friend," he said.

"Why are you even here?" Mr. VanDoren asked, pointing at me.

"*Harold*," Mrs. VanDoren chided him, but he ignored her. "Jim is Anne's life. More than we are—"

"You've never actually cared about her," he cut her off, eyes only for me. "If you did, then you would've tried to reconnect with her sooner. Not wait until she came home, vulnerable and broken—"

"She's not broken!" I snapped. "And you're one to talk. You tried to set her up with Brad for the same reasoning you're accusing me of!"

"Take that tone with me again, young man," he said. "I dare you."

"*Nah*," Ridge's voice sounded from behind me, slightly out of breath like he'd ran up the stairs too. I didn't know who texted him, but I was suddenly so fucking grateful to have someone here who was on my side. "Pump the brakes, old man," he continued, stepping up to shove us away from each other.

"Who the hell are you?"

Ridge glared at him, then shook his head. "Don't care," Ridge said, turning his back on him and looking at me. "What do you need?"

"I just wanted to make sure she was okay," I said, defeat crashing over me. His daughter was unconscious for fuck's sake and he was wasting time with this bullshit?

Ridge gave me a nod, turning to face the family. "Let him see her."

"No." Mr. VanDoren's voice was final, lethal even.

Ridge took a step toward him, but I placed a hand on his chest. "It's okay," I said, looking at Anne's father as I lowered my voice so only he could hear. "You think you'd be more concerned about your daughter's well-being and happiness instead of a decade-old grudge against a sixteen-year-old. You have no idea who I am anymore. I don't even think you know who your daughter is."

"And you do?"

"Yeah," I said. "I do."

"It's sad," he said. "How highly you hold yourself. Do you honestly think you're worthy of a daughter like mine?"

"I love her—"

"Love her," he cut me off. "Love her? You said the same thing all those years ago and where did that get you? Where did you two end up?" He glanced around the waiting area. "Look at where we *are*. Do you think you're giving her some grand life?"

Where did we end up? Where did that get us? *Jesus*, this man. He would never approve of me, never stop fighting me at every fucking turn. If it wasn't for him, we would've stayed together. I knew that in my bones. If he hadn't pulled us apart, Anne's life would look a hell of a lot different, we'd proven that over these last few weeks. Proven what life could've been, but he wanted to shame me? He wanted to keep me from her again?

I curled my hand into a fist, seeing nothing but red—

"Easy," Ridge's voice said into my ear as he pulled me back.

I was shaking as he continued to walk me back toward the stairs. Farther away from Anne, farther away from assurance that she really was all right.

And as her father watched me with that same hatred in his eyes, it all compounded inside of me—ten years of not being good enough, of not living up to an impossible standard. No wonder Anne had lived the way she did. Nothing was ever good enough for him.

It never would be.

That truth clanged through me like the ringing of a bell.

Nothing would ever change.

And I was an idiot for thinking it would.

"Come on," Ridge said, guiding me through the stairwell

door. "We'll get answers," he said as we descended. "Just, when you've cooled down."

I nodded, letting him lead me back to the main floor lobby, where Lyla was waiting for us, waters in hand.

I chugged mine then shook my head. "I'm going home," I said, utterly defeated. "As long as he's here, he won't let me near her."

My entire world felt like it was crashing down around me, the love of my life lying in a hospital bed with no way for me to get to her while her father was standing guard like a deranged protection detail.

As if *I* was a threat to her.

As if I didn't love her more than he could even fathom.

As if I didn't have a ring in my pocket right this very second, begging to slide onto her finger and claim her as mine forever.

CHAPTER 17

Anne

"Jim?" My mouth was so dry it made it hard to say his name.

Memories come rushing back to me as I opened my eyes, the action like trying to lift a damn car. The smell of sanitizer hit my nose right before I registered where I was.

A hospital room.

I was hooked up to an IV, solution dripping slowly down the tube. I blinked a few times, remembering the events at Lyla's. I felt exhausted, then the pain...then nothing.

I glanced around the room, expecting to find Jim asleep in a chair next to my bed, but it was empty.

"Hi, Andromeda," a pleasant female voice said as she walked into my room. "I'm Jillian, your nurse."

"Hi," I said, forcing myself to sit up in the bed.

"How is your pain right now?" she asked, checking my IV drip before wrapping a blood pressure cuff around my other arm.

I did an internal check, relieved when the pain from my

memory was nowhere to be found. "A two," I said. "I'm a little groggy."

"That would be the pain relief medication we administered when you first arrived," she explained, nodding as she took my blood pressure and then removed the cuff. "Along with some antibiotics," she said. "You had an infection from fluid buildup around your liver, but your levels are stable now."

"Damn," I said, blowing out a breath. "Is anyone here?"

"Your mother and father are just outside. Your sister too, I believe. There were a few others here last night, but they had to leave since they're not family."

That explained where Jim was, even though he was more family to me than my own at most times.

"Do you want me to send them in?"

"Can you give me a few minutes?" I asked. "I need to make a call before I can handle..."

Jillian gave me an understanding look. "I got you," she said. "The doctor will be in to check on you in about fifteen minutes anyway. I'll see how you're feeling then, all right?"

I nodded, and she headed out the door.

I grabbed my phone that rested on the small table next to my bed, expecting to see at least a few texts or missed calls from Jim, but there was nothing.

Dread settled heavy in my stomach, but I hoped that had more to do with me waking up in a hospital than him not checking on me. Surely, he was fine, right?

I dialed his number in a hurry, panic flashing through me about something terrible happening to him on a call or an accident or—

"Hello," he answered, his voice cold and low but relief still barreled through me at the sound.

"You're okay," I said.

"Are you?"

"I'm fine, I think. I just woke up."

"That's good."

"That's good?" I asked. "That's it?"

"It's really good, Anne. I was worried about you."

"Then why aren't you here?" I asked. "Surely the visitation can't be that strict. Tell them you're my boyfriend—"

"It's not the hospital's fault," he said. "Your father threw me out."

"What?"

"Yeah," he said, his tone all wrong. He sounded angry and defeated and something else I couldn't figure out. "He wouldn't let me see you. Then proceeded to blame your entire situation on me and then—"

"Hey," I cut him off. "We all know my father is a real dick," I said. "That has nothing to do with you not being here. I'm in the *hospital*."

"Anne, I know. I've never been so scared in my life when Lyla called."

"Lyla called you?" I asked.

"Yeah, your boss called me. Not your family. Your father was shocked I was even there."

"And that's why you're not here? Because of him?"

Jim sighed, and I could almost picture him pinching the bridge of his nose. "He wouldn't let me see you," he said again. "He practically banned me from the entire hospital."

My heart sank into my stomach, a sense of unworthiness washing over me.

"You're a grown man," I said, anger and hurt coloring my tone.

"What?"

"You are a grown man," I repeated, tears forming in the backs of my eyes. "Hell, you're a police officer, and you let my father keep you away?" I shook my head, tears rolling down my cheeks.

"He wouldn't let me—"

"Fuck him, Jim!" I snapped, my entire heart breaking in two. "I would've fought. I would've raised hell if someone had tried to keep me from you." I sucked in a sharp breath. "But that's always been our problem, hasn't it?" I swiped at the tears on my cheeks. "I'm not worth fighting for. I never have been and I clearly never will be."

"Anne," he said my name like a prayer, but it did nothing to stop the ice forming around my heart.

"Goodbye, Jim." I hung up the phone before he could say another word, and crumbled into a million pieces, sobs tearing out of me.

"Anne," Sephie's voice was kind and supportive as she hurried to my bedside, wrapping her arms around me.

"I'm never going to be enough," I cried into her shoulder, clinging to my sister like she could help hold me together. "I have way too much baggage."

"Shh," Sephie hushed me, smoothing back my hair. "I know that's not what Jim said."

"He may as well have," I said, shaking my head as I tried to take deep breaths to get my shit together. "He let Father push him around—"

"I wasn't here for that," she said. "I jumped on the first plane out here."

"You didn't have to do that," I said. "I'm fine."

"I can see that," she said, arching a brow to indicate the legit hospital bed I was in.

I laughed a dark, broken laugh, and she joined in.

"What if it's true though, Sephie?" I asked. "What if I really am never enough? What if I'm not worth the fight?" I shrugged. "I guess it would be pretty fitting though, right? I've been a terrible person. I treated you like shit for years for a situation you had nothing to do with," I said. "In what world should I be allowed to have someone like him love me?"

179

"Oh, I guess I should've worn my cocktail dress," Sephie said.

"What?" I asked, gaping at her.

"For your pity party," she shrugged at my shocked look. "Well, you are," she said. "Because you know that is *nonsense* about not deserving his love. And I told you I understood the strain between us, even if you couldn't elaborate."

I'd explained to her that something had made me act out against her, but that it had nothing to do with her and everything to do with me a couple of weeks ago.

"You're working through your past, Anne," she continued. "And it has no power over your future. Not unless you decide it does."

I straightened up, giving her an apologetic look. "I'm sorry."

"It's okay," she said. "I'm all for wallowing in misery if that is what you need, but I don't really think it is."

"It isn't," I said. "I'm just..."

"Upset," she finished for me. "Understandably. But most of that blame needs to go to our father."

"I know—"

"Hello, Anne," the doctor said as he walked into the room, my chart in his hand. "You gave us quite the scare there."

My father and mother followed him into the room, and it was all I could do to not go off. I wouldn't cause a scene though, for *once*.

"Your levels are stable now, and the antibiotics are doing their thing. We'll have to monitor you for another day, but then we should be able to discharge you. And our visits will go from bi-weekly to weekly, but I think you're going to come out of this really well. You just have to stick to your medications and *eat*."

"I understand," I said. "Had I forgotten to take my meds?"

"We're pretty positive you did," he said. "Set a reminder in your phone. Multiple ones if need be. It even helps if you give your schedule to family and friends for reminders too."

I'd given my schedule to Jim weeks ago when he'd asked and he'd never failed to text me with a reminder. But yesterday had just been crazy and I'd forgotten to take it even after he texted.

And now...

Now he wasn't even here.

My heart sank all over again.

"Thank you," my mother said as the doctor headed toward the door.

"Not a problem," he said. "The nurse will be back in to check on you in a little while. This wasn't your fault," he added as he lingered in the open doorway. "You're doing remarkably well. One of my best patients to date." He smiled at me before heading out.

My mother instantly hugged me, worrying over me the same way Sephie was. It felt genuine, if not a tad bit awkward. I can't remember the last time we hugged like this. And when they released me, my father tried to hug me, but I stopped him.

"Andromeda?" he asked, backing away at my urging.

"I've made every change you've requested of me," I said, and the tone in my voice must've broadcast to the room that I meant business, because Sephie and Mom got off my bed and headed toward the door, lingering there for support but giving us our space too. "Every single demand you placed on me when I returned home and asked for help. I've done them and more. I've found myself with the help of therapy, I've been sober since the day I asked Sephie for help. I've stayed out of trouble, I completed the volunteer work you found for me, and I do a damn fine job at *Lyla's Place*."

"I know," he said. "And I'm proud of you."

Nothing. Not even a flicker of happiness rolled through me at his words. "I don't need your approval anymore," I said, and his eyebrows shot up his head. "Or your attention. I've done the hard work on my own, and trust me, digging through my trauma *is* really hard work because there is a lot of it. But the one thing I need from you, you probably won't give me."

"Andromeda—"

"And that's some goddamn credit," I finished.

Sephie fist-bumped the air behind my father, and I had to bite back a smile at her support. My mother nodded encouragingly.

"I don't know what you mean," he said, completely flabbergasted. I think there might have even been a bit of hurt in his eyes, but I couldn't really tell.

"You know exactly what I mean," I said. "You don't trust me to make the right decisions, and fine, maybe I made that bed these last ten years, but even before that you didn't trust me. You still pulled Jim and I apart—"

"This is about him? You were teenagers!"

"I was in love!" I fired back. "And I *still* am."

He stumbled back a step, his mouth hanging open.

"I love Jim. He sees me in a way no one else ever has. He is the *best* man I've ever known and he inspires me to be the best version of myself. And if you trusted me at all, you would trust that what I say about him is the truth. You wouldn't be treating him like some bad business deal not worth your time." I sighed, years of anger rushing through me. "And for the record, you can keep your inheritance. I've been living just fine on my own for the last couple of months, and I know I can do it forever. I'd rather live a life with Jim than have all the money in the world. So you have *nothing* to hold over my head any longer."

Sephie shifted her weight near the door, a smile on her face that mirrored my mother's.

Real, genuine pain flitted over my father's face, and it stung but not enough for me to say I was sorry. I wouldn't apologize for telling the truth.

"I'm..." He opened and closed his mouth a few times. "I'm sorry."

Shock slammed through me. I wasn't sure I'd ever heard those words come out of his mouth before, definitely not when directed toward me.

"I need you to let me talk now." He took a cautious step toward my bed, like he was approaching a wild animal. "I've made a lot of missteps in my life, Andromeda," he admitted, and the words made emotions tangle in my throat. "But my biggest one has been with you." He visibly swallowed. "I never wanted to hurt you," he continued. "I was trying to protect you. I thought I knew what was best for you when I should've trusted you to show me. I almost lost your mother, and then, when the doctor told me you wouldn't make it a year if you kept at it..." He shook his head. "That made me hold onto you even tighter."

Tears rolled down my cheeks.

"The demands were my attempt to keep you here with us."

"I'm not ungrateful," I said, my voice cracking. "I just need you to accept and love me for who I am." I looked at Sephie, then my mother, then back to him. "Which is not my sister. Or my mother. I will never be them," I said, the admission cracking open something inside of me. "But I will be me. Unapologetically. And I'm going to surround myself with people who accept that. You can decide if you're one of those people or not."

"I am," he said quickly. "Oh, honey, I am. I hope you'll give me a chance to make this up to you. I didn't mean to make you feel this way, and maybe I need to take some of my own advice and get help too. I will. I promise I will."

He reached for me, and I nodded, allowing him to hug me. It was stiff, but I wrapped my arms around him too, letting the sincerity of his words register.

"We should talk more," Mother said. "Look at what holding everything in does to a person."

I laughed through my tears, rolling my eyes as I shared a look with my sister. Holding things in had been what we were raised to do—as all proper southern ladies were.

But not anymore.

She was right.

It was better to let it out.

And to let it go.

CHAPTER 18

Jim

I was happily ignoring reality, petting Binx on my couch with all the blinds drawn when a pounding at my front door scared him off. He scurried out of the living room, retreating to his tree post thing in the other room.

"Some guard cat you are," I chided him, not bothering to get up. I didn't want whatever anyone was selling.

"You're not even answering the door anymore?" Ridge's voice sounded through the entryway, and seconds later he rounded the corner.

"I don't want company."

"Tough shit," he said, sinking down on the chair opposite me. "You look like shit too."

"Thanks."

"It's been two days, man," he said.

"Is that all?" I asked. It felt like a month had passed since I left the hospital. Since Anne called and told me what an asshole I'd been, what a coward I'd been for not fighting for her harder.

"Are you going to get up and fix this shit with your girl?"

he asked. "Or are you going to make me give you one of those rom-com pep talks?"

I cocked a brow at him. "You don't do pep talks."

He shrugged.

"And I can't," I said. "She deserves a life where she doesn't have to justify who is in it. Doesn't have to battle her father at every turn. She deserves someone with endless wealth and possibilities—"

"Yeah," Ridge cut me off, leaning over the coffee table between us and snatching the engagement ring I had sitting there. "You're right," he said, nodding as he examined the ring in the box. "She wasn't ever really worth the hassle anyway," he continued, and I furrowed my brow at him. "Putting up with all that upper society, VanDoren popularity bullshit would be a nightmare. No woman is worth all that—"

"She is," I snapped, standing up because the adrenaline was too much to take sitting down. "She's worth *everything*," I said. "You're my best friend, but I will knock you the fuck out if you keep talking about her like that."

Ridge smirked as he stood up, staring at me with a knowing look.

"Oh," I said, shaking my head. "I'm a fucking idiot."

"Yep."

"I need to go."

"I'll drive," he said as I tossed on some shoes and we both headed to the door.

I swung it open, stopping dead in my tracks.

Mr. fucking VanDoren himself stood at my door, hand poised like he'd been about to knock.

Ridge moved to step between us, but I waved him off.

"What are you doing here?" I asked, trying like hell not to plow him over and head to my car. It was New Year's Eve, and I knew Anne was healthy enough to work at Lyla's because

186

Persephone had been keeping me in the loop despite everything.

"Talk with me?" he asked, motioning to my front porch.

I nodded, following him outside. Ridge pretended not to watch us through my closed screen door.

"I owe you an apology," he said, and I about rocked back on my fucking heels I was so shocked.

I didn't say a word though, just folded my arms over my chest and stared him down.

"A big one," he continued. "I had no idea that my actions all those years ago were the wrong ones. I had no idea how real the love you two had between you was. You were teenagers, I thought it was a fleeting thing."

"It wasn't."

"I know. And I know I shouldn't have continued treating you the way I did when you came back into her life all these years later." He shook his head. "It's not an excuse, but when I found out she'd die if she kept up her ways...I was terrified. I almost lost my wife, the idea of losing my firstborn..." A shudder ran the length of his body. "I thought if I controlled every facet of her life, then I could keep her safe. Keep her here with us."

"And I wasn't part of your grand plan."

"No," he admitted. "You weren't. But I was the asshole for thinking she needed me to control her life in the first place. For being arrogant enough to think I knew what was best for her." He pressed his lips together. "She set me straight, trust me. She even told me she doesn't want my inheritance. She wants nothing from me, except for the respect she's owed."

That's my girl.

Pride swelled in my chest.

She finally stood up for herself.

"I won't lie to you. The main reason I'm here has more to do with me wanting to mend things with my daughter than ask for forgiveness. But be that as it may, will you accept my apology?" he asked.

"On one condition," I said.

"Name it."

"I'm on my way to see her right now," I said, stepping into his space. "Are you going to stand in my way?"

A slow, accepting smile spread across his face, and he took one large step to the side, clearing the path to my car.

I gave him a nod, and before I could even turn around, Ridge was there, shaking the ring box in one hand and his keys in the other. "I've got what we need, let's go."

Mr. VanDoren tried to nod at Ridge, but he shook his head.

"Nope, still don't care," Ridge snapped, not even bothering to look at him as he headed to the car.

I shrugged, following him.

I heard Mr. VanDoren laughing as I got in the passenger seat, and Ridge took off toward what I hoped would be the start to the rest of my life.

CHAPTER 19

Anne

Nothing like working on New Year's Eve after a little siesta in the hospital to make you feel human again.

Lyla's was wall-to-wall packed, and I practically had to beg her to let me take my shift tonight. She was terrified, my poor friend. I'd given her a real scare, but after showing her the discharge papers from my doctor and promising her I would take breaks and do better about eating, she allowed me to come in.

And I was enjoying myself, I had to admit. Everyone in the place was alight with joy and the prospects of the approaching new year. I was too, the idea of a fresh start stretched out before me with an array of endless possibilities.

So many of the pillars in my life were falling into place. My family—coming to terms with my father being the biggest leap. My friends—Lyla and Brad had become the best friends I'd ever had outside of Jim. My health—my liver was healing, just like my mind, my soul. I was still very much a work in progress, but progress was being made.

There was just one thing not aligning like I wanted, and that was my heart.

I missed Jim.

I missed working with him and laughing with him. Missed the way he made me feel, missed doing everything I could just to hear his laugh.

But he hadn't called, so I hadn't either.

Because where could we go from here? Had I come to terms with my father? Sure. But that didn't change the past and it certainly didn't change the present. Too much damage had been done, and even though I knew it was a pity party, I couldn't help but think I was more trouble than I was worth.

"Happy New Year," Brad said over the roaring of the chatty crowd as he made his way over to where I lingered by the front counter. I was taking a quick break since all my tables were okay for the moment.

"Happy New Year," I said.

"How are you feeling?"

"Great, actually," I said. "I thought I wouldn't bounce back as quickly but it's amazing what the body can do when it isn't in a constant state of hungover."

Brad laughed, shaking his head. "Humor," he said. "That's a good sign."

"I try." I glanced around. "If you're looking for a table, you're out of luck."

"I'm good," he said. "I'm actually heading to Luna's for an after-midnight party. It's kind of our tradition, but I just wanted to pop in and check on you first."

"Don't lie," I chided him. "You're here for those." I eyed the samples on the counter, and he shrugged, popping one into his mouth.

"Can't it be both?" he grinned at me, and I laughed, reaching up to swipe a stray piece of cake off his immaculate suit.

"Lunch next week?" I asked, and he nodded, giving me a quick hug.

I released him, and he headed toward the door...

Where a very jealous looking Jim stood, an even grumpier looking Ridge behind him.

Brad raised his brows at me, a silent gesture if I needed him to stay, but I waved him off. He smiled and headed out the door, Ridge barely budging an inch to let him by.

"Is he your date for New Year's Eve?" Jim asked once he made his way through the crowd.

"Why?" I asked, heart racing at the sight of him. Sweat heavens, he looked downright sinful in a pair of black athletic pants and a gray T-shirt. "Would that bother you?"

He stepped so close to me I could feel the heat coming off his body. "It would, seeing as you're still mine."

Warm shivers danced down my spine at his words, at the look in his eyes. "Am I?"

"You always have been," he said. "I've loved you since we were sixteen. I love you now. And I'll love you when we're sixty, too."

My heart climbed up my throat.

"I don't care if I have to fight every single day to remind you how amazing you are, how fantastic and funny you are. I don't care if I have to fight for my place at your side. I'll do it. Because you're worth fighting for, Anne. You're worth everything. And on the days you don't think you are, I'll just love you that much harder."

Happy tears rolled down my cheeks, and he swiped them away, reaching in his pocket and pulling out a small box, opening it between us.

"What do you say?" he asked as I stared at the gorgeous ring inside the box. "Want to take it one day at a time with me forever?"

My heart leaped, the answer crystal clear.

"Yes!" I threw my arms around his neck, and he caught me against him, hauling me off my feet and spinning me around.

The crowd started the countdown, the place reaching ear-shattering levels of loud.

"Three, two, one!" the crowd shouted before erupting into applause. Cheers rang out all around us as the band Lyla hired shifted to Auld Lang Syne.

"Happy New Year, baby," Jim said into my ear before kissing me senseless.

"Happy New Year, *James*," I said, holding my hand out so he could slip the ring on my finger.

"Do you think Lyla will notice if you disappear for a little bit?"

I shook my head. "I think we can spare a few."

Anticipation raced through me as Jim took my hand, leading me through the crowd and through the back of the restaurant until we came to the little supply closet. I opened the door, practically shoving him inside before locking it behind us.

It was small and cramped but it was private and that was all we needed.

"I love you," Jim said against my lips as he pressed me against the door, lifting me until I locked my ankles around his back.

"I love you," I said right back, kissing him frantically as his hand plunged beneath my skirt. He tore the hose I wore underneath, the primal action sending liquid heat pulsing down the center of me. "Hurry," I demanded, a sense of urgency spiraling through me.

He shifted his weight, freeing himself before he lined himself up with my center.

"Say it again," he demanded, teasing me with the tip of his cock.

"I love you," I said again, breathless as I clung to him.

He plunged inside me, filling me up so fast and hard I gasped for breath.

"I love you so fucking much," I said again, and he rewarded me with another thrust.

Then another, each one setting my insides on fire.

"Fuck, you feel amazing, baby," he said, pumping into me as he supported my weight against the door.

I kissed him, licking into his mouth and relishing the feel of him inside me.

"Don't ever leave me again," he demanded, pumping into me at just the right angle to hit my aching clit. "You're mine now. You feel this?" he said, grinding against me for emphasis.

My eyes rolled back in my head as I tried to stay grounded to this planet, but it was so fucking hard when he pumped into me like that.

"I get to make you feel this good forever," he said, joy and claiming surrounding his tone.

Pleasure worked its way up my spine, spiraling in warm tendrils along every inch of my body.

"Forever," I agreed, the word sounding like the sweetest thing I'd ever heard.

"We're short on time, baby," he said, kissing me as he thrust in again. "You're going to come for me now." He ground against me again before pumping into me fast and hard, my body bouncing from the motions as he drove me into oblivion.

"James!" I cried out, my orgasm making me clench so hard around him he found his release inside me at the same time.

He kissed me, hard and claiming. "Such a good fucking girl."

I shivered and stood corrected. *Those* two words were the sweetest to hear, and I never felt more loved or seen in my entire life.

We quickly cleaned ourselves up, hurrying back into the crowded restaurant before anyone noticed our absence. Well, Ridge may have, with the look he shot us, but he kept himself busy annoying the hell out of Lyla, if her agitated face was any indication.

I checked on my tables, grateful that they weren't in need of a thing, and did my best to finish my shift with my fiancé intently watching me the entire time.

Sweet heavens, my *fiancé*.

I was going to marry the love of my life.

And no one on this earth could stop me.

Epilogue
ANNE

One month later

"**A**re you sure you don't want to at least tell Mom?" Sephie asked me as we looked through the dress racks at Luna's Boutique.

"I'm sure," I said, smiling at my sister. She'd carved out time just for me to dress shop, and it was truly wonderful how natural it felt. We were sisters again, with nothing between us but love, and it made a world of difference. "We'll tell everyone else once we've been married for a while."

"I'm glad you told me," Sephie said, grinning at me as she held up a dress and I shook my head. She placed it back on the rack. "Eloping. How romantic."

"Yes," I said, practically swooning. Life with Jim was already so amazing it already felt like we were married. "While your wedding was breathtaking," I continued. "We don't need anything big. We just want it to be the two of us. Maybe a few years down the road we'll have a party or something but for now, this will be perfect."

"I'm with you," she said. "I loved my big wedding, but

there is something to be said for fast, secretive weddings in Vegas."

I laughed, heading to look at another rack. "I mean it worked out for you, right?"

"That it did," she said, holding up another dress, this one a simple black that would match my ring. I certainly wasn't going to wear white, not when I'd worn white to all the others.

This would be the last wedding, the one that mattered.

"Oh!" I said. "That's definitely the one!"

"Yay!" Sephie squealed as we did a happy dance.

"Pray it fits!" I said, crossing my fingers as I hurried to try it on.

It fit like it was made for me, and I came out to show Sephie, who was talking with Luna when I came out of the dressing room.

"Wow," they both said at the same time, making me smile even more.

"You look gorgeous," Sephie said.

"It's like I made it for you," Luna offered, and I smoothed my hands over the dress.

"You're seriously so talented," I said.

"You two are some of my best customers," Luna said as I headed back into the dressing room and changed out of the dress. "I never knew weddings could be my thing!"

I laughed as I came out, fully dressed in my own clothes. "Well, I'll definitely be buying this one."

She took the dress from me with a smile. "I'll get a garment bag and meet you at the register."

Sephie and I browsed a bit more while Luna headed to the counter, her door chiming with another customer.

"Brad!" I was shocked to see him here and from the look on his face he was as equally surprised to see me.

"What are you doing here?" he asked, giving me a quick hug and following me and my sister to the counter.

"Can you keep a secret?" I asked.

"You know I can," he said.

"I'm buying my wedding dress," I said, and Sephie gaped at me. "He already knew," I explained and she pretended to be offended for a second.

"Did Luna make it?" he asked, his deep tenor curling around her name.

"I did," Luna answered him, nothing but snark in her tone.

"Well then I know it's perfect," he said, grinning dramatically at Luna. "Because she would never *ever* let anything hang in her shop that she didn't spend hours working on, even forgoing events she promised to go to—"

"Enough," she laughed, rolling her eyes at him. "And before you ask again, the answer is *no*," she continued.

"You're going to change your mind," Brad said, his blue-gray eyes scanning her face with a sort of determination I'd never seen from him.

"What are you doing, Brad?" I asked as I gave Luna my bank card. "Proposing to Luna to get a discount on custom suits?" I joked.

"Ha," Luna laughed, handing me back my card. "I charge him extra."

Sephie and I chuckled at that.

"No," she continued. "Bradly dearest is trying to rope me into a scheme of epic proportions and I'm simply not here for it."

He smirked, sliding his hands into his pants pockets. "Come on," he said. "It'll be fun, Luna. Just like old times."

"Never. Going. To happen." She handed me my dress, but I didn't budge an inch. Neither did Sephie. We were invested now. "Plus, I'm pretty sure my boyfriend wouldn't be into the idea."

"Like I've ever cared what he thinks," Brad said, a muscle

in his jaw flexing before he smoothed the look with his normal, charming smile. "You'll change your mind," he said. "You always do." He turned to me, pointing to the garment bag in my hand. "That's going to look beautiful on you, Anne," he said before he winked at Luna. "Take care."

He headed out the door, and I stared after him for a few moments before turning back to Luna.

"He's ridiculous," Luna said, waving toward the door. "He always drags me into the most ludicrous situations."

Sephie and I looked at her expectantly. "And?"

"And," Luna said, chuckling. "This time I'm putting my foot down. There is no way I'm pretending to be his fiancée on a business retreat for some company he's trying to buy just so he can be included in all the couple stuff with the owners." She shrugged. "A girl has to draw the line somewhere."

"Wow," I said, pursing my lips. "I had no idea Brad was so…"

"Into role playing?" Luna offered, and we all laughed at that. "He has a good heart," she continued, a kind of wistful look in her blue eyes. "But sometimes he doesn't think about how other people have boyfriends, lives to live, shops to run, and dresses to make." She nodded toward the dress.

"Happily ever afters to facilitate," Sephie added, and Luna smiled at that.

"I do what I can," she said. "I'd love to see a picture of you in it after the event."

"You got it," I said, my phone buzzing to remind me to take my meds. I left my water in the car, so we had to book it. "Thank you again! And good luck with Brad!" I called as we headed out.

"I don't need luck," she called back. "It's not happening!"

We laughed as the door closed behind us, and I got into Sephie's car, hurrying to take my pill on time. I'd been really good about it ever since I had the incident last month.

Jim: Did you take your meds, baby?

Me: Yes, dear.

Jim: Good girl.

"Wow," Sephie said, turning onto the road.

"What?"

"You're looking at your phone like you want to devour it," she teased. "Whatever he said, I don't want to know."

Jim: You coming home to us? Binx is insufferable right now.

Me: On my way.

Jim: Love you.

Me: Love you back.

I put my phone back in my bag, unable to stop smiling.

"Okay, fine," Sephie said. "What did he say?"

I looked out the window, watching the town as we drove toward my new home. "That he loves me."

"That's it?" she teased. "That's what has you smiling like that?"

My heart expanded in my chest. "That's all I've ever needed."

THE END

Thank you so much for reading! Are you you new here and curious about Anne's sister Persephone? You can read all about her and Cannon here!

Craving a billionaire romance? Check out what happens when the owner of the NHL Carolina Reapers agrees to let a romance author shadow him for a novel she's working on! You can find it here!

. . .

Want to start at the beginning of the Carolina Reapers? The NHL's been at Axel's door since he was eighteen, but he'd never leave the Swedish hockey league while he was raising his little brother. But now he's grown, and the Carolina Reapers are at Axel's door with his greatest weakness: Langley Pierce. The fierce and fiery publicist has sworn off men, but if she wants him to accept her proposed contract, she'll have to accept his...proposal. Read Axel, book one in the Carolina Reapers series here!

Can't get enough sports romance? NFL quarterback Nixon Noble hasn't been able to forget—or find—the woman he spent an earth-shattering night in Vegas with...until Liberty shows up with the ultimate shock—a pregnancy test with two pink lines. Their chemistry is undeniable, but he's bound by contract, and her post-masters dream job is a continent away. Read Nixon, the first book in the Raleigh Raptors series here!

If you love these alphas and want to try something with a little more bite, check out my steamy vampire romance, Crimson Covenant!

Connect with me!

Text SAMANTHA to 77222 to be the first to know about new releases, giveaways, & more!

Text VAMPIRE to 77222 to get all the paranormal news first!

Sign up here for my newsletter for exclusive content and giveaways!

Follow me on Amazon here or BookBub here to stay up to date on all upcoming releases! You can also find me at my website here!

Acknowledgments

I want to give a MASSIVE thank you to YOU the reader. I seriously couldn't do this without you and I'm so honored that you love these series and characters as much as I do! Thank you times a thousand!

Thank you to my incredible husband and my awesome kids without which I would live a super boring life!

Huge thanks must be paid to all the amazing authors who have always offered epic advice and constant support! Not to mention creating insanely hot reads to pass the time with!

Big shout out to A.H. for making this shine. And thank you to each and every single one of you AMAZING readers who love the these books as much as I do!

About the Author

Samantha Whiskey is a wife, mom, lover of her dogs and romance novels. No stranger to hockey, hot alpha males, and a high dose of awkwardness, she tucks herself away to write books her PTA will never know about.

Made in United States
North Haven, CT
17 August 2023

40403074R00124